TWISTED VOWS

A Deadly Marriage of Lies and Revenge.

By Sara Kate

PART 1

1

Lily's Getaway

Three awful things happened to me in less than a month. My mother died. My little brother tried to steal my car. And I found out my husband is cheating on me.

Last week was the car incident with my brother. The week before, my mom's burial and yesterday, I found out about my cheating husband, Jordan. Hearing his phone conversation with his mistress last night was my last straw.

So, I hopped on a plane to get away from everything for three days. But how stupid was I for trading Miami's scorching ninety-degree weather for New York City's miserable bitter cold, twenty degrees. I don't even know a single soul in this state. I left one city to go to another—an even shittier and bigger city.

I just wanted to get away from my life. I wanted to get away fast. And I did. My destination, however, could have used a bit more thought before I booked my flight.

Miami has its flaws but it is not exactly the greatest and safest place to live either. At least Miami has better weather than New York does though. In Florida, I can walk outside in a bikini without anybody questioning my sanity or freezing my ass off.

Stupid, stupid me for choosing to come here. This might be one of the reasons why my husband is cheating on me. I'm impulsive. When I finally decide on something, I make a thoughtless and irrational abrupt decision without thinking about the outcome or consequences of my actions.

While questioning my life choices, my taxi escorts me from the airport through the busy streets of New York to an overly expensive hotel somewhere near Central Park. When I booked my hotel room on a whim this morning, right after I booked a flight to get here, I decided that since I have the money, I might as well splurge on something extravagant.

Now, I wish I didn't. I should have chosen a staycation back home in Miami instead. I could be sleeping at a different hotel, one that costs half as much as the one I am heading to right now, with a nice view of the beach only inches away from the sand tonight. Instead, I chose to trap myself in a large building surrounded by hundreds of people for the next few days. That is, unless I want to step out into the cold weather.

A staycation would have been a *much* better option. But of course, rage blinded my critical thinking and now, here I am in the cold.

When I caught my husband talking to his mistress on a video call at home last night, I chose not to confront him. Fury took over my emotions and I just wanted to get far, far away from him. Far away from everything. Away from work. Away from my own house. *Just away.*

New York City sounded like a good idea in the moment because the flights weren't too expensive and I always wanted to see what the city was like. Now that I am here, the idea is not as appealing to me anymore. It's the middle of February. Why is it so damn cold here?

Then again, as a born and raised Floridian, how the hell would I know what the weather would be like? I should have googled the weather but of course, I did not think that far ahead. Blinded by rage and my impulsiveness once again.

The time is 6:15 p.m. No call from my soon to be ex-husband yet. Jordan, the cheater should be almost home from work by now.

Jordan owns a moving company called SoFlo Miami Movers, with two other partners, Levi and Richard. They celebrated their three-year business anniversary just last month. During the past year, Jordan has worked overtime *too many times*. Or so, I thought he did. Now I know where he really was.

The thought of his countless lies; every time he said he needed to stay at work late because he is a partial owner of the company, nag at me like a fly buzzing around my ear that is impossible to catch. Although Jordan and his business partners are not movers themselves, Jordan told me they all still show up to the office five days a week for whatever reason that was never understandable to me until now. Now I know, he was probably never at the office. He was fucking someone else.

He said he would be home by six o'clock today. Looks like he was lying because my security camera app on my phone has not alerted me of any movement outside of the house yet. Oh, how I wish I was there to see his reaction in person when he walks through the door to an empty house!

Okay, admittedly, I'm being a bit dramatic. The house is not *empty*. It's not like I took everything I own with a plan to never come back—although, the thought did cross my mind, but I did leave with a small suitcase that will last me for three days. And Jordan has no clue where I am until he gets home tonight!

As a manager at a twenty-four/seven diner, it is not very professional of me to just not show up to work without calling, so I told my boss I had another family emergency and I'd be gone for three days, counting today. After ten faithful years of working at the diner and since my mother passed away recently, my boss had no room to deny my request of absence. This time, my family emergency consisted of my brother's mental state of mind. My boss thinks Mike; my five years younger brother, had a mental breakdown and I had to go take care of him.

I might not always think my decisions all the way through but at least, lying comes easily to me. Whether my lies are believable or not are debatable. Either my boss believed me or he took pity on me. Either way, I'm free from work for the next few days.

The cold breeze stings my cheeks when I step out of the taxi and in front of a huge fifteen-story hotel that I was starting to regret booking until now. The beautiful double glass door entrance of the building wipes away all my pessimism. I have never stayed in a place this extravagant. Might as well enjoy my time here. After all, that's the reason I booked this place. To pamper myself. To give myself some *me* time. To forget about my daily stressful life. And most of all— to forget about my cheating husband.

Even though it is freezing outside, I can still spend my days inside, enjoying room service without caring about the outside world. The snow is pretty to look at from the window. No need to stand on the white slippery ice especially without winter boots and a winter jacket. I wanted to see the city and now I'm here. I've seen enough of it on the drive from the airport to the hotel.

After checking in and settling into my luxurious hotel room, the security camera app buzzes on my phone, alerting me of movement outside my house. Finally, there goes Jordan walking through the front door. An hour past the time he originally told me he'd be getting home, might I add.

In a moment, he will notice I'm not there. He probably thinks I'm home because my car is still in the driveway. An Uber took me to the airport this morning, so I wouldn't have to pay an absurd amount of money it costs to store my car at the Miami airport for three days. Yes, I said I didn't mind spending on my *me trip,* but the car storage would have been overkill. And my car is safer at home anyways.

And like clockwork, my phone rings, removing the live image of my view of my doorstep and front yard off my screen, replacing it with Jordan's name and his smug cheating smile. I swipe ignore on his call. Time to tap into my *me time.*

Several images of killing my cheating husband come to mind as these silky black bed sheets hug my body in this perfectly made king-sized bed. I imagine how I'll get my revenge once I am back home in Miami. Different scenes play out in my mind; one of them involving the crystalized chandelier hanging from the ceiling above my head. I wish we had a chandelier over our bed at home. I would cut it from the ceiling and let it fall on Jordan while he sleeps. Glass would shatter all over, prodding his body, the weight of the chandelier enough to impale him.

But that beautiful gruesome image disappears when my phone buzzes with a new text message.

From Jordan: Honey, where are you? I tried calling but you're not picking up.

I begin typing, *I'm several miles away, thinking about ways to kill you.*

Then I hit delete and lock my phone.

2

An invitation
entirely in her
favor

After ignoring Jordan's text, he called me four times. I thought about turning my phone off to really make him sweat but I decided lying to him would make me feel better. Hell, he's been lying to me so now it is my turn!

"I drove to my brother's this morning. I just got here about an hour ago. He's still really depressed about my mom. I'll be back home on Wednesday in the afternoon," I lie to Jordan over the phone.

I am not sure how long the dead mom card can be used for, but right now, it seems like a good excuse to use as to where I am. There is no way Jordan will figure out I'm in New York because I used my own secret savings account to pay for the plane ticket and hotel. As far as he thinks, I am only about five hours away from him. Not a couple states over.

My mother overdosed on painkillers a month ago. It's not like none of us saw it coming. She became addicted to the pills after her third back surgery two years ago. It was only a matter of time until abusing the pain pills finally caught up to her. Mike and I didn't have a great relationship growing up. Not with our mom or with each other. It wasn't until a few years ago when my brother and I started to become cordial with one another. We would call or text each other once every few weeks, but I guess that was better than not talking at all. It was not until my mother's funeral when we saw each other in person for the first time in about seven years.

"So does this mean you're not mad at Mike anymore?" Jordan asks with disdain in his voice. He has never been a fan of my younger brother, despite only meeting him recently. And after we caught Mike trying to steal my car in the dead of night shortly after they met, that disdain grew stronger.

"I can't be mad at him forever. He's been struggling with mom's death. You know he was drunk that night we caught him outside. It's not like he consciously knew what he was doing when he tried to steal my car. Not that I am defending his actions, but it's a good thing we woke up and stopped him from taking it or else he could have ended up in a grave with my mom too."

Really, I am still livid with Mike which is why we haven't spoken since the incident. Waking up at two in the morning to see my drunk brother attempting to hotwire my car with another drunk idiot friend of his was not a fun sight to see while I was half-asleep. I plan to talk to him eventually. Just not until after I get back home and decompress from my impromptu getaway.

"I guess you're right," Jordan says. "But I'm surprised you just decided to leave without telling me first. You didn't even say goodbye to me before you left. What about work?"

"My boss knows how bad Mike's been doing so she gave me the next few days off. I wasn't thinking and just left once he called me. I figured you'd be working late again tonight, so what would it matter if I left when I did? I didn't want to do the five-hour drive at night. That's why I left this morning after you went to work."

Mike lives up the coast in Jacksonville. Five hours away. Not too far away, yet not far enough away from me. He was only down in Miami when he tried stealing my car because he went to a music festival that night.

"Okay, you're right. Well, tell him I said hi. I miss you already," Jordan says.

Sure you do.

"Will do," I respond.

"Oh, by the way, Richard and Levi invited us to go on a camping trip in the keys next weekend. It's sort of an early celebration for Richard's birthday next week," Jordan says just as I am ready to end the call.

"Oh... Okay," I say.

"Wanna go?" he asks.

"A camping trip? You mean, we'll be sleeping in a tent?" I laugh at the idea of sleeping outdoors. We've never done that.

"Yes, dear. We'll all have different tents. Besides you and me of course."

"Who else will be there?" I ask because it's odd that they invited me on a guys trip.

"Just Levi, Richard, and Gia."

Gia. That's Jordan's mistress! That's the bitch my husband is fucking. I heard him say her name on their video call right before he abruptly hung up when he heard me walk into the backyard. That was my first clue he was cheating before even hearing the bitch's voice; he took a call privately in the backyard. Away from me. He never does that.

"Who is Gia?" I try to hide the suspicion in my tone. It is not easy.

"Richard's fiancé," Jordan answers in a tone that suggests I should have known that already.

When did Richard get engaged? My husband is cheating on me with his business partner's fiancé? No way! Jordan wouldn't betray his business partner and so-called best friend—Wait... what am I thinking?

Yes, he would! Of course he would! He's betraying his own wife of fifteen years, so what would be the difference?

And besides, I *know* what I heard. Jordan said Gia's name right as I opened the sliding door to our backyard where they were having their secret conversation. Then he hung up. I know what I heard. I heard Gia's sweet soft slutty voice.

She sounded skinny. Blonde. I am guessing about ten years younger than me. Unlike me—a thirty-five-year-old with pronounced frown lines, flabby triceps no matter how often I try to work them out, and pale skin even though I live down the street from the beach. But in my defense, when work takes up all my time, going to the beach becomes less of a priority, no matter how close the ocean is to me.

"Lily?" Jordan's voice breaks me from my thoughts of sticking a knife in both Jordan's and Gia's eyes. I imagine she has blue eyes. Blue and blonde; the perfect combination. Complete opposite of my appearance and physique.

I want to say no to going camping next weekend but then again, this little trip could work out in my favor.

What a great place to kill somebody— on the beach at night in the dark when nobody else is around. Sounds like a cinematic setting to get my revenge... a perfect place for retaliation.

"You know what? Sure!" I answer. "Sounds like a lot of fun, honey. Can't wait!"

3

3 Days Later

Three days of staying in New York made me realize that I should never take being a Floridian for granted.

Snow sucks. It's pretty to look at and to stand in for about five minutes. Other than that, the snow is agonizingly cold. The slippery ice sucks too. The only hoodie that I brought from Florida did absolutely nothing in regards to shielding me from the northern weather. And even with a thick winter jacket that the weather forced me to buy at a store next to the hotel, I still froze. Turns out keeping myself prisoner in an extravagant hotel room gets boring after a day. I tried venturing around the streets which is when I bought the jacket. I only lasted outside in the weather all of twenty minutes before rushing back to the hotel.

I will never come back to New York, ever. The only upside about this trip was leaving my husband and forgetting about my life for three days. No dishes to wash. No floors to vacuum. No laundry to get done that is not mine. Nobody to manage at the restaurant. No needy customers to satisfy.

I expected my adulterous husband to invite his secret bitch over to our house while I was gone, but according to my front door camera, nobody came to visit. The only person who walked in and out of my house while I was in New York was Jordan. He strolled into the house just a few minutes past nine o'clock every night.

He had to have been with that bitch, Gia. He normally leaves his office around five in the evening on the rare occasions he isn't *working late*. Traffic in Miami is terrible, but not terrible enough that it takes four hours to get home. Two hours at most, depending on how many accidents occur on I-95. Four hours is pushing it unless the road is completely shut down due to a crash or construction.

I checked the news. No big accidents occurred over the last two days. There were no shut down roads. No new construction that hasn't already been occupying the roads for as long as I can remember. My cheating soon to be ex-husband took advantage of my absence and he stayed out longer to be with his bitch the past two nights. *I know it.*

When he called me this morning as I was packing up in the hotel to head to LaGuardia Airport, I asked him what he did after work while I was away. He told me he ordered pizza, drank a few beers, and watched a movie before going to bed. *Liar.*

Another overly expensive taxi escorts me to LaGuardia Airport to catch a flight back to my hometown; the beautiful, sunny and excruciatingly hot Miami. After my twenty-minute adventure in the cold the other night, keeping myself locked in the hotel room with endless amounts of wine made me think about our upcoming camping trip in the Keys next weekend.

Oh, the endless possibilities I will have to get my revenge.

I am not sure how I will execute the kill yet, but I know for a fact, I will commit a murder on the sand, and the weekend can't get here any sooner.

4

Islamorada, Florida Keys. Camping trip - Day 1

The Florida Keys is a beautiful place especially Islamorada; a village located in the middle Keys. Islamorada is just about two hours away from Key West itself which is in the lower keys.

Driving into the Keys was scenically peaceful as we drove over the ocean and the mangroves. The drive itself was not so peaceful for my intrusive thoughts though. The sudden image of any four of our tires blowing out and the car suddenly swerving off the road, then plummeting into the water appeared in my mind an unhealthy number of times. I'm glad the trip was planned here in Islamorada because if we had to go any farther, then we would've had to drive over the seven-mile-long bridge to get all the way down to Key West itself. *No, thank you.*

After an almost two hour long trip of sitting next to my cheating husband as he swerved around numerous cars on the highway, a margarita by the ocean is all I desire. Especially before I meet the bitch who is fucking my husband.

I've visited the Keys, including Islamorada a few times years ago, in my twenties before. I have never been to this little desolate beach where we're currently setting up our tent though. Correction— where Jordan is setting up our tent. While he does that, I'm going to the small airstream trailer that has been turned into a mobile bar. The cute little bar is not so conveniently parked at the entrance of the parking lot, far away from where we're staying.

For some reason, Jordan decided the perfect place to set up camp would be at the end of the beach, at least a quarter mile away from our cars, the bathroom, and most importantly, this lovely bar that is about to become my best friend for the weekend.

Besides the scenic view out here, the bartender is pretty nice to look at too. Better looking than my cheating husband is. I haven't been to a bar in a long time, probably in about over two years. You would think that would be impossible since I live in Miami, a world-renowned party city, but I am not in my twenties anymore. I have no time or desire to hit up a crowded club or a bar. Not with my husband. Not with my employees or coworkers. Not with any friends, not that I have any. And definitely not by myself either.

While sipping my frozen twelve-dollar salt rimmed, tequila margarita (Jordan is going to flip when he finds out the price of this delicious drink), I begin the long trek back to camp. If I had known where Jordan would set us up, I would have stopped here first before following him the whole way.

On my way back toward him, a young couple who look to be in their mid-twenties, drag hefty beach chairs and a camping bag across the sand right past me. Their two little rascals run ahead of them. As the woman yells the children's names—Linda and Roslyn, I can tell that she needs a drink too. This is one of the times that I feel grateful for never having children. Kids would hinder my murder plan during this trip. I can't have any distractions this weekend.

With my delicious margarita in hand, I begin to feel less unnerved. The stress of watching my husband swerve in and out of traffic while dodging numerous accidents on the highway along the way here is beginning to leave my body. I must say, even though Jordan is a cheater, a deeming worthy quality about him is his impeccable driving. He dodged so many horrible drivers on the way here and kept us safe, so I'll give him that.

"Hey! Over here!" Jordan calls out as I finally reach our tent. I could kill him just for simply choosing to set us up all the way at the end of the beach. I've already downed nearly half this drink just on the walk back.

It's obvious he isn't waving at me since I can clearly see him so I turn around and see three people: Levi, Richard, and a woman. A strikingly attractive woman, might I add. Heading toward us, the three of them are coming from the direction of where the parking lot and the bar is.

That woman is not only stunningly slender, tan, and toned, but she looks very *young* too. She looks like she can't be much older than twenty-five. She's already in a bright pink, skimpy bikini with no cover-up and she isn't blonde as I expected, but brunette instead—the same color as my hair is. Except her hair has more bounce to it than mine and it's much longer than my shoulder cut length. The strands bounce against her back as she walks and of course, she's a bangs type of girl. Long voluminous wispy bangs flow across her forehead. Red lipstick. Barely any blush. Barely any makeup at all.

I knew it. Perfectly good flawless luminescent skin. Not dull or pale. No wrinkles either. Unlike my forehead which is in desperate need of Botox with my ongoing sagging neckline, hidden beneath layers of my foundation.

When the group gets closer, my attention shifts over to Jordan's business partners. I have only met Levi and Richard a handful of times over the years. Even though they are Jordan's business partners and best friends, there has been only three occasions when we were all in the same room together; The day they opened their moving company, then there was a time when I came to visit the office shortly after their grand opening, and the third time was during a small celebration they had for their three-year business anniversary not too long ago.

As they approach us, Richard's hand rests across Gia's lower back. I catch a glimpse of my husband's reaction. He either doesn't notice or he is pretending he does not care about their relationship very well.

"Glad to see you three made it here alive!" Jordan greets them with that universal handshake and slap motion that guys do with each other. Gia smiles at him, says a quick hello, but other than that, they do not acknowledge each other.

How subtle.

"Just barely made it here. Too many idiot drivers in South Florida," Richard huffs as he dramatically drops two heavy bags on the sand. One of them looks similar to the bag that Jordan pulled our tent out of. "Did you really need to pick this spot man? What a long ass walk!"

"Gia, this is my wife, Lily." Jordan has the audacity to introduce us as I sip my emotional support drink.

How dare he!! I hate introductions. I hate socializing. I do enough of acting phony with people at work.

"Nice to meet you." Gia offers a hand out toward me. "I'm Richard's Fiancé."

I reluctantly remove my margarita from my lips and plaster on a fake smile. *Fiancé. You didn't need to tell me that. Your fancy big diamond ring was enough of a tell.*

"Nice to meet you too." I shake her hand, tapping into my hospitality work personality. *Damn, her hands are even softer than mine are.* Everything about this woman is ten times better than me.

"Where'd you get that?" Levi points to my half drunken margarita. "I need a beer after that drive and this walk. Jordan, why'd you have to pick such a far spot to set up?"

"I wanted to be far away from people," My husband shrugs.

"Well, you did a good job," I mutter before turning my attention to Levi. "There's a mobile airstream bar near the parking lot. You guys walked right by it." I point toward a sand path in the mangroves that is a few feet ahead of us. The sandy path leads all the way back to the parking lot.

"I brought a cooler full of beers and tequila for us, man." Jordan gestures to his cooler.

"Well, let's save all that for tonight. I don't mind paying overprice for a brewski right now. Might as well live in the moment while we're here," Levi shrugs. "I gotta take a piss anyway."

"I guess you're right," Jordan mutters.

I know he wants to sulk about it though. He doesn't like paying over price for anything and he also does not like any type of confrontation. Unless the confrontation is with me while he's drunk.

"Can you get me a margarita like Lily's, honey?" Gia asks Richard.

And suddenly, the three men are heading down the trail. The nerve of my husband to leave me alone with his side bitch! I could kill him right now!

Another sip down. Two more sips to go and my drink will be gone.

"Honey, grab me another one of these too!" I shout to Jordan.

He turns around and raises his eyebrows at me. Not sure if he is judging me for already nearly gulping this entire drink down or if it is because he doesn't want to pay for another one. Or maybe he is giving me that look for both reasons.

They say opposites attract and it's true. My very social husband is the complete opposite of my introverted self. Although I work in hospitality, I could not be more of an introvert. Managing twenty servers and tending to about a hundred or so customers daily is enough for me. Outside of work, I like to keep to myself which is probably why I don't have friends. That would be another reason why I think my husband decided to cheat. I'm not enough of a social person for him. And also, just look at Gia. If I had the chance and I was a guy, I would cheat on me with her too.

"Oh, my God. We must've dodged about ten accidents driving down here," Gia brushes a brunette strand away from her cheeks and fans her face with a tiny pink fan that she suddenly materialized out of one of her bags.

Here she goes with the small talk.

"Yeah. Us too," I mumble.

After briefly fanning herself, she gracefully moves on to pull out a tent from one of the bags Richard carried over here.

And even worse, other than being so attractive, to even more of my surprise, she begins setting the tent up only a few feet next to ours! All by herself! She's even an outdoorsy woman. This perfect woman is just full of surprises, isn't she?!

There goes another trait she has that is totally opposite of me. This is my first time even seeing a tent in person. I have only ever seen them on TV and on social media. I did not even attempt to try and help Jordan set ours up, not that he needed it. Surprisingly, he set our tent up quickly and with ease. Just as Gia is doing.

As she sets up the tent, my eyes shift over to look inside the other bag she brought with her. There's a Glock case in there. Jordan carries the same type of handgun in his car. He didn't bring his gun out here to camp though because he always leaves it in the glove compartment. Sometimes, he brings it in the house. Whenever he remembers to take it out of the car, that is.

I wonder if the Glock is hers. Or the gun could be Richard's. I've never heard my husband say anything about Richard owning a gun. Then again, Jordan rarely ever talks about Richard or Levi to me. We rarely speak about his company and partners because honestly, his business is not that interesting. The few times we eat dinner together doesn't normally include talking about my job or his company anyway. Mostly, we end up watching TV or a movie while eating. Sometimes we talk about family—at least family has been a topic of conversation lately, after my mother's passing and since my idiotic little brother tried to steal my car.

"That yours or Richard's?" I nod toward the gun case.

"Oh, it's mine. Richard doesn't carry a gun. I didn't want to leave my gun in the car in case it got broken into. The parking lot is pretty far out of sight from here. I saw a few other cars parked out there, so I figured there must be other campers on the beach with us. And there were no streetlights in the parking lot from what I could see, so I just wanted to be cautious, you know? I wouldn't be a responsible gun owner if I left my gun unattended and God forbid it got stolen and put into the wrong hands."

"I get it," I nod. *God forbid.*

"You got a problem with guns?"

"Oh, no. Not at all," I say because I don't. But I do have a problem with *her* owning one. I have shot my husband's Glock a few times at the range when he first bought it. I just don't own a gun myself because I have never felt the need to carry one since he has one to protect us. Now my feelings about my safety have changed after seeing this tiny woman proudly owning the same Glock herself. Why should I rely on Jordan to protect me? He's not *always* with me.

"My husband carries a Glock too," I say.

"Oh yeah, I know." Gia flaunts her perfectly whitened teeth in a smile. "Me and Richard have spoken about going to the range with him before. It just hasn't happened yet."

Of course they have. Wait, why the hell would she think I have a problem with guns? I find that rude and judgmental.

Then again, it's probably because my husband doesn't talk about me at all. Typical. Why talk about your wife to your own mistress?

Last sip down. I can move on to my second drink now, but it is taking an awfully long time to get here.

As I watch this woman navigate the tent setup process with ease, I realize Gia is only half of what I imagined. She's more. She's skilled in things I am certainly not. She does not come off as fragile despite her appearance. Even though she is obviously skinnier than me, I am not much stronger than her, given her toned arms. She does not seem to show any doubts in her shooting capabilities either, which is not good for me.

I can shoot a gun but I am not proficient or highly skilled at it. The last time my hands were on Jordan's gun was when he first bought it two years ago and he took me to the range. If I had to defend myself in close quarters, I would not think twice about shooting a close-up target. Far away would be more of a challenge for me.

The sight of Gia's gun makes me rethink my life choices. If only I owned one just like hers, especially during this weekend.

But Jordan has the same one tucked away in the glove compartment of our car that is only about a ten-minute walk away.

Up until now, I had no idea how my murder plan would get executed out here on the beach. But thanks to Gia, I now have my answer.

5

Islamorada, Florida Keys. Camping trip - Day 2

Sleeping outdoors was not as bad as I thought it was going to be. Maybe it was because we weren't sleeping directly on the ground. Jordan set up an air mattress with a bunch of blankets on top of it, so our sleeping arrangement inside the tent was actually quite comfortable. Not that I thought sleeping in a tent would be a *terrible* experience. It's not like I am a high maintenance woman. Sleeping on the ground isn't below me. Camping is just something I never had the desire or opportunity to do.

Between the countless number of margaritas I drank last night before Jordan cut me off around a sixty-dollar bar spend (what a cheap ass), the sound of the waves crashing against the shore and the breeze coming off the ocean helped me sleep well too. He's lucky the air stream bar closed at 11:00 p.m. or else I would have fought him on the limited bar spend he put me on. Tequila shots and beer are not my thing. I have no idea what I would do if that airstream bar wasn't here. Normally, I am a wine or a margarita type of woman. Jordan seemed to have forgotten about that when he packed the cooler.

After this weekend, I think I'll go camping again—without my husband and his mistress.

If it weren't February, I would be mad about the long walk I just had to do to go to the bathroom. The breeze out here and temperature drop (a cool seventy-five degrees which is basically winter for Floridians) made the walk from camp pleasant though. Putting on my makeup was a number one priority before anyone saw me this morning. Including my husband who is already helping Levi cook our breakfast. There was no way I was going to go makeup free while breathing the same air as Gia today.

"Morning!" Levi says while cooking breakfast on the portable grill.

The aroma of eggs, sausage, and bacon fills the air. Until now, I hadn't thought about any of us eating this weekend. I guess Levi must have brought the grill with him because Jordan didn't and I did not see it in Richard's and Gia's bags yesterday. Next to the grill is a cooler full of frozen burgers and hotdogs. The guys must've divided up duties for the weekend. Jordan was in charge of drinks, which he did an exceptional job of doing for himself and the guys while Levi apparently supplied the food.

There are three other tents on this beach, including the stressed young couple with their two little rascal children. All of which we haven't met yet and probably will not talk to either because they're set up so far from us. Everyone is dispersed at least a thousand feet away from us, closer to the parking lot and bathroom.

I cursed Jordan for setting up camp so far from everything, but his lack of foresight actually ended up working out in my favor.

It's a good thing nobody is near us. This way, when a dead body turns up on the beach, nobody will know how or what happened to the person because nobody is close enough to witness anything. This is perfect.

6

Islamorada, Florida Keys. Camping trip - Day 2

"What are you doing?" Jordan's voice echoes behind me.

Shit, he caught me. My murder plan is already getting screwed up before it even started. This is probably because I didn't have a well thought out plan to begin with. I only had a goal—to end a life. This is just another example of how my brain works, how I make thoughtless decisions without thinking about the consequences or outcome. Seeing Gia's gun planted the image of using Jordan's gun in my head and since I know where he keeps it, I went for it.

But Jordan caught me before I could get my hands on it.

"Honey?" Jordan stands behind me as I am hunched over the glove compartment in our car.

I should have known my husband would look for me out here in the parking lot since I was gone so long. I told him I was going to the bathroom which was true, but I ran to the parking lot afterward.

I back myself out of the car to see Jordan standing behind me in the dark parking lot where ours, Richard's, and three other cars are parked. There are only three spaces left open in the lot. Gia was right about there being no streetlights out here. If the Keys were prone to burglars, I'd be worried about a gun getting in the wrong hands too.

"Did you forget something in the car?" Jordan asks.

Hmm, what *did* I forget?

Not my makeup because he saw me take my makeup bag to the campsite yesterday when we got here and he watched me take it to the bathroom this morning. I also came back with a full face of foundation, lipstick, and mascara. Not sure whether he noticed my appearance or not though. Probably not. Still, I won't take any chances.

He knows I don't have my period right now so using the *looking for tampons* excuse is out. I can't say I'm looking for my clothes because he grabbed our bags out of the car yesterday when we first arrived here...

"Lily? Why aren't you answering me? Gia checked on you in the bathroom and didn't find you, so I figured you went back to the car. Are you okay? What did you forget?"

Fucking Gia. Of course she is the reason he caught me out here.

"I didn't forget anything. I was looking for your gun," I say.

"What? Why? Why would you need my gun?"

"Don't worry about it."

"Don't worry about it?" he scoffs. "Are you kidding me? Why would you suddenly feel the need to look for my gun?"

"Because... what if, what if we need it for protection? Like what if a wild animal comes on the beach while we're sleeping? I heard weird noises last night," I say.

"We're on a beach in the Keys. It's not like sharks are going to jump out of the water and attack us on the sand. There are no wild animals out here. The deer are even harmless." My husband, the wise guy.

"So then where is your gun? I thought you brought it with you. It's not in the glove compartment where you normally keep it."

"It's in the tent. In a bag. I took it out of the car when we got here yesterday."

"Okay, well then let's go back to the campsite." I close the driver's side door behind me. The light inside of the vehicle dims seconds later.

Jordan and I walk alongside each other through the small dark parking lot back toward the stretch of beach. He stops at the edge of the parking lot before reaching the sand.

"So, since when do you just grab my gun without telling me? I don't mind, but I'd prefer that you ask me before grabbing it on your own," Jordan says.

"I'm not a child. I know how to handle a gun."

"I know, honey. It's just odd that you went to look for it without telling me. Since when do you do that?"

"Since I found out that you're cheating on me." *Fuck. I wasn't supposed to say the quiet part out loud.*

Too late.

"Very funny." Jordan shakes his head.

When he goes to walk by me to head toward the beach, I grab him by the back of his shirt. "I'm not laughing."

He turns around. "What the hell? You're actually serious right now?"

Look at that smug smile on him. I want to shoot it off his face with his own gun.

A single nod of my head causes my husband to drop that arrogant smirk when he says, "I'm not cheating on you. Wait... What does that have to do with you looking for my gun?"

"Because... because I planned to shoot somebody tonight."

7

I said the quiet part out loud

"W—what? You don't mean... you don't mean you were going to *shoot me,* were you?" Jordan's eyes widen; a look of terror and confusion plasters his face.

"No. Although I thought about killing you a few times, I could never go through with it. I'm going to kill your mistress instead."

"My who?" Jordan laughs. The grin is back. He thinks this is a joke.

"Your mistress," I repeat. "You heard me."

His smirk starts to disappear. Seems like he's beginning to realize this isn't a joke after all.

"I don't have a mistress. I just told you I'm not cheating on you. I never have. Never will, honey."

"Then why were you on a video call with Gia the day before I went on my trip—I mean, before I went to visit my brother?"

I almost let my impromptu getaway last week slip. It nearly slipped my mind that Jordan still doesn't know I was in New York for three days. And he won't ever know where I really was as long as I do not accidentally blab about it. Thankfully, I've always had a separate savings account from our shared checking. I never had to use the money in my savings account for anything until I booked my little getaway. As far as Jordan knows, I was with Mike in Jacksonville.

Speaking of Mike, I should eventually call him to see how he's doing.

No, fuck that. He should call me and apologize for trying to steal my car.

Jordan's face turns grim. "Gia? That's who you think I'm cheating on you with? You know Gia is Richard's fiancé."

"No, I did not know that until you told me recently. I don't know anything about your business partners. But I *do* know that I heard you talking to Gia privately on the phone in the backyard last week. When I opened the backdoor, you hung up quite quickly. You never take calls outside away from me. You were being sneaky and you got caught."

"I wasn't being sneaky. I just wanted fresh air when she called. And I didn't hang up because you walked outside. The conversation was already done. You walked out when we were hanging up," he says.

"Oh, was it? Because I heard her say she couldn't wait to see you at the bar. Then you hung up as soon as you realized I walked outside."

"No, she said she couldn't wait to *go to the* bar, not to *see* me. Everything else you heard was true but I'm not cheating on you with her! We were talking about meeting at a bar because we were planning Richard's birthday party for next weekend. We had to go to the bar to talk to the manager and check out the place so we can schedule his surprise party. Look at this video." Jordan pulls his phone out from the pocket of his shorts, then scrolls up on the screen for a few seconds before turning the phone toward me.

"See? These are pictures of the bar and if you play this video, you'll hear Gia talking to the manager in the background while I take a video of the place. I was recording so we can figure out where we're going to put the decorations. Gia's idea, by the way. I don't give a shit about the décor. She wanted me to take the video in case Richard saw it on her phone. She knows the bar owner and apparently, they go there every weekend. She's planning to rent the place out next Saturday night for his party."

As I watch the video and tell him to shut up so I can hear the little bitch talking to the manager in the background, I confirm he is actually telling the truth. They really were meeting at the bar to discuss planning Richard's party.

"When did you two go there?" I ask while reviewing the video again.

"Last week, when you were visiting your brother. That's what you heard us making plans to meet about."

Oh, so that would explain why Jordan was gone for so long during one of the nights I was away. But that does not explain where he was the second night... unless he actually did work late and the traffic was terrible coming back home. If he worked until seven, then yes, coming back two hours later around nine o'clock at night is plausible...

And if he were cheating on me with Gia, he wouldn't be stupid enough to show me this video. I can hear Gia's soft annoying voice all giddily while she converses with the manager about planning Richard's birthday in the video. This means the phone conversation that I heard between my husband and her makes sense... Perfect sense. But why did they have to be on a video call to discuss?

Still, only mildly satisfied with this video evidence, I scroll through his gallery while his phone is still in my hand. There are more photos of the bar. No naked photos of Gia, thank God. None of me either. Not that I've sent him any in probably a couple years. No naked photos of any other women for that matter. If he were cheating with her... or with any other woman, then there would be some form of sexting on his phone, I would think. Then again, I wouldn't know because I am not a cheater. There are no other conversations though his text messages either. Not even a text thread with Gia. I guess they've been conversing on calls only.

Well, fuck. Don't I look like an insecure woman now.

"Why did you have to be on a video call with her?" I ask.

"Does that matter? She called me that way and I answered her. Didn't really think too much into it. I can't believe you thought I was cheating on you," Jordan lowers his voice. "Wait... were you, were really going to shoot her with my gun?"

"Yes," I shrug.

"Holy shit!" Instead of sounding shocked, Jordan lets out a laugh.

"Why is that so funny to you? You don't think I'm capable of killing someone?"

"Oh, I do think you're capable, honey. I'm just glad you weren't planning on killing me. And I'm glad I caught you out here before you got your hands on my gun. I can't believe you were going to shoot Gia. She's a nice woman. Richard's smitten over her."

I will not admit to him that I didn't plan on shooting Gia until I saw her gun and I realized that I could kill her with my own. Well, not my own. Clearly, I thought I could have used Jordan's. I wasn't thinking of the consequences or cleanup afterward. Or the loud noise a gunshot makes. Even though the other campers set up their tents far from us on the beach, they would still probably hear a gun shot.

Well, I guess it is a good thing my husband caught me out here after all then. If he hadn't shown proof of the party planning on his phone, I wouldn't believe him when he said he isn't cheating.

But I do believe him. Of course I do. Why did I get that suspicious so quickly after that one phone call? My husband wouldn't cheat on me! Sure, we've had some distance between us over the last few months because of our work schedules and the stress of losing my mother and my idiotic brother being more present in my life, but Jordan cheating? No way! We have spent sixteen years together, fifteen of those married, and we've never had any reason to question each other's fidelity. Why on earth would I think such a thing now?

It must be because my self-esteem has dwindled lately— a realization I am just now coming upon. I literally heard a woman's voice, even worse on a video call, who I've never heard before and automatically assumed my husband stopped loving me. Why didn't I ask him about his conversation? I just assumed! When the hell did I become so insecure?

I could blame my new emotions on my mother's death, the guilt of not being close with her until recently, and the stress that has endured because of it. My age could also play a factor in my feelings too. Turning thirty-five six months ago hasn't been such a breeze on my body and my mind. All of a sudden, I have been more focused on whether it's time to get Botox or just age not so gracefully.

Well, damn. If I'm letting my age mess with my mindset now, then what the hell is going to happen to me when I hit menopause... in how many years? Ten or twenty? Doesn't perimenopause start around age forty? That's in only five years...

Let me quit thinking about woman problems while I'm ahead. Back to what's important; Jordan's gun.

My husband never carries his gun on him. It's always either in the car or in the house. Never actually with him in public. So why take it to the tent? He said it himself, what would we need protecting from? There aren't thieves around here.

"So why did you bring your gun inside the tent then? You always leave it in the car," I ask. "You said it yourself, there are no wild animals lurking around. So... what's your reason for taking it to camp?"

"Because..." sighing, he grabs my arm and leads me back toward our car.

"What are you doing?" My voice rises an interval.

"Shh," Jordan whispers, tightening his grip around my wrist.

"Nobody can hear us over here!" I retort. "The campsites are so far from here, the tents look like ants."

"Ants? You're so dramatic. They're like five hundred feet away from here."

"You know what I mean!" I sigh.

Jordan leans against the driver's side of our car and exhales. "You weren't supposed to know about my plan."

"About what plan?" My eyebrows furrow. What kind of mind games is he trying to play right now?

"I plan to get rid of Levi tomorrow night."

"Get rid of... get rid of, as in *kill him?*"

8

Oh, how the tables have turned

My husband nods.

Now it's my turn to laugh at Jordan. There is no way we both came out here with a plan to murder two separate people. Jordan must be messing with me because of what I just told him.

"And why the hell would you want to do that?" I ask in disbelief.

"Well, because Levi deserves to die for being a piece of shit and then we can cash in on a life insurance policy on him," Jordan answers, his expression as serious as I've ever seen it.

Did I just hear him correctly? The smirk that was once on his face is gone again. Life insurance? What life insurance? Why is Levi a piece of shit?

"Honey? Did you hear me?" Jordan shakes me by the shoulders.

"Are... are you joking?"

"Were you joking about wanting to shoot Gia with my own gun?" He tilts his head slightly.

"Well, no... but–"

"Okay. I'm not joking either."

"Why do we need money so badly? We're financially fine." *At least, I thought we were.* "And what life insurance policy are you talking about? When did you take out a life insurance policy on him? How is that even possible?"

"No, we're actually not financially fine," Jordan sighs.

My husband has taken care of all the bills for as long as I can remember in our marriage, but we shouldn't be broke. I've had a stable salary over the years. I even got a raise last year just like I do every year. Only a few cents each time, but it still adds up on my paycheck. Jordan's moving company has had a steady amount of clientele from what he's told me. The only debt we have is our mortgage of about twenty-five thousand dollars left to pay off. We just paid off our last credit card not that long ago too.

"Why? What's going on with our finances?" I ask.

"I had to open a new credit card to cover a sudden expense at work. Richard and Levi don't know about it because I fucked up with a client booking. I applied for a new credit card in my own name, not under the company. If I don't pay the card back, then we're going to end up broke by next year. If I wait, the interest rates will increase and I'll never be able to get rid of the debt."

I was expecting Jordan to tell me something far more sinister than needing to get out of sudden credit card debt. I was expecting him to say something like a customer who belongs to the mafia or some type of drug lord is blackmailing him and refusing to pay for his moving services. Maybe he was going to say a loan shark was after him. Something far more dramatic than wanting to pay back a credit card.

I can't help but laugh. Uncontrollably laugh. Hands on my knees, bent over, tears forming in my eyes— kind of laugh.

"Lily, this is not a joke! I'm not kidding!"

"S—sorry," I try to catch my breath and wipe the tears from my eyes. "Whew! Oh, that was a good laugh. Sorry, I just thought you were going to say something much worse than credit card debt. What did you do that you messed up so bad with a client booking? I don't understand what you needed to open a credit card for. How much do you owe on the card?"

"I had to buy some new equipment for the movers for the client. Don't worry about what it was. I owe a couple thousand dollars."

"How much is a *couple* thousand?"

"Ten thousand."

"What cost ten thous—?"

"—Don't worry about it. Listen, if Levi or Richard die, then I get a big enough payout from the life insurance policy afterward because I'm a beneficiary. When we started the business, we all took out life insurance policies on each other to cover business expenses in the event that one of us die. When I kill Levi, Richard will get a portion of the payout from the insurance with me because he's also one of his beneficiaries, but there will still be plenty of money to pocket for ourselves. Enough to pay back the ten thousand and have some cash left over."

"How much in total would you get for the policy?" I ask.

"Fifty-thousand."

"Okay... but—but why are you planning to kill Levi and not Richard? Are you really that desperate to pay off a credit card because you're scared of high interest rates?" I cross my arms.

Jordan says this isn't a joke but it sure feels like one. At least, I had a valid reason for wanting to kill Gia. I thought she was a home wrecker trying to destroy my marriage. That is reason enough to kill a bitch. Being in debt for ten thousand dollars is not a reason to kill someone though.

"Because like I said, Levi is a piece of shit. He also doesn't have any beneficiaries on his policy besides Richard. Other than me, that is. Richard has Gia on his so I would get less money than I will when Levi dies. But that's not the only reason. I want to get rid of Levi because he deserves it. He was abusing his ex-girlfriend, Sharon. They broke up last week. She came into the office with bruises all over her body and told me that Levi almost killed her and her twelve-year-old daughter. She showed me pictures of her daughter's arms all bruised too," Jordan sighs.

"She only came into the office to tell me how much of an asshole Levi was to them and that she finally left him. She wanted me to know what kind of guy my business partner is. Richard was there too when she showed up. I never met her until that day, but I did see pictures of her on Levi's phone so I knew she wasn't lying about who she was."

"Where was Levi when she showed up?" I question him.

"Levi wasn't in the office when she came in. He told me they broke up a few days later. No mention of abuse or anything, but I knew Sharon told me the truth. Levi has always had a temper. I've seen it come out at work. He also told me they argued a lot. He would call her obscene names in conversation with me and Richard. He'd talk trash about her daughter. It was disgusting to hear."

"You never told me any of this," I give him a look of skepticism.

"I didn't want to. I didn't even want to hear the things Levi told me. They were together for a couple of years," he says. "Toxic relationship. More toxicity on his end than hers."

Jordan has only known Levi and Richard for five years. They became friends at the gym two years before they decided to go into business together. Since my husband is a natural extrovert, it made sense one day when he came home from the gym and told me about his new business idea with two strangers I had never met before. Jordan had been working at an office for several years before then and he was tired of the corporate world, so I supported his decision to become an entrepreneur. He came up with a business plan, executed it rather quickly, took out a few business loans between the three of them and started up the moving company a few months after the idea came to fruition.

I wouldn't know if my husband is lying about Levi being an abuser because I don't know anything about the guy.

Did Jordan come up with all this on the spot just to cover up the fact that he is cheating on me? Maybe his mistress isn't Gia. Maybe it's another woman.

Or have I officially lost my mind along with my self-esteem? After all, I was ready to commit murder without planning out how to actually kill a person first. But could my husband do the same? Plan a murder and go through with it?

Well, yes... I think so. I can picture him killing someone if he really had to. He's never had a temper with me. During arguments, he has yelled a few times especially when he drinks, but he's never laid a hand on me. Although, if he has a good reason to kill another person, which seemingly he does, I can see him getting the job done. I should hear the details of his whole murder plan before I decide whether or not he is bluffing though.

"So you were just planning to shoot Levi with your gun out here?" I question him. And yes, I am very aware of how hypocritical I sound right now. Sure, my plan to kill Gia with his gun is basically the same as his plan, but my decision came to mind on a whim. Clearly, Jordan has had more time to think his own strategy through. And let's not forget, I am an impulsive person especially when I'm blinded by rage. Thinking rationally goes out the window for me.

"No. Shooting him is my backup plan. I'm going to make his death look like he drowned himself in the ocean after I get him drunk by the fire tomorrow night. I just grabbed the gun as a precaution. In case the plan went sideways," Jordan answers.

And by the look on his face, it's clear, none of this is a joke after all. He really came to the Keys to murder his partner.

My husband is capable of murder.

Shit, and so am I. Regardless of whether I was going to be good at it or not.

Even after fifteen years of being married, sixteen together in total, I guess it is possible that we can still surprise each other. As the saying goes, true love never really dies. Especially when both people are just the right amount of unhinged as we are.

I lean against the door of our car, smiling. "Well, how can I help you kill him then?"

9

A Walmart version of Bonnie & Clyde

We have resorted to sitting in our car in the dark per Jordan's suggestion.

If he wants to be inconspicuous, maybe sitting out here in a dark car past midnight is not such a good idea. Then again, nobody can see us from the beach and since it is so late, everyone is probably asleep already. Levi, Richard, and Gia should be inside their tents by now since we all called it a night right before I slipped away to the bathroom and snuck out here.

If anything, if someone knows we're sitting in the car, then maybe they'll think we're having a fight. Or having sex. To them, either one could be plausible.

"You want to help me kill a man?" Jordan scratches the back of his head while he looks at me, bewildered.

"Of course I do. You're my husband, after all."

"Yeah, but you thought I was cheating on you." He furrows his eyebrows.

"And I was ready to kill the home wrecker because *you're my husband*. I still love you. That didn't mean I wasn't angry with you though. Like I said, I imagined killing you a few times. I wasn't mad enough to actually do it though. I could never shoot you. I figured we could work through our problems. I only thought you were cheating on me because you were making plans to meet another woman at a bar. Wouldn't you think the same way if you heard me make the same plans with a man?"

Jordan shrugs. "I-I guess."

"How could I have known you were talking to Richard's fiancé? I didn't even know he had a fiancé. Hell, I didn't even know Richard's birthday is next week."

"I didn't have a chance to tell you about his party because you left to see your brother last week. I didn't think about the party until now. I was too focused on this weekend. Of course I was going to tell you about the party. I planned on bringing you," he smiles. "Even though I know you would rather stay home."

"You know me so well," I smirk. "So do Richard and Gia know about your murder plan?"

"No, not at all. This was all on me. I'm not even sure if Richard knows about how the payout works after one of us dies. We took policies out on each other but that was early on after we opened the business. He probably doesn't even remember doing that. I heard a guy at the gym talking on the phone to an insurance company about a claim he filed after his business partner died from a heart attack. That's when I came up with the idea to get rid of Levi. This was right after Sharon talked to me in the office." Jordan leans back in the driver's seat.

"Between the debt for the expense I owe on the new credit card and Levi's shitty behavior, I decided killing him just seems right. Richard has no idea that I planned this weekend just to kill Levi. Inviting him with Gia and you on this trip made for the perfect cover up. So that way, I won't be the only suspect. You'll all be my alibi. We're all going to be each other's alibis."

How smart of Jordan to use his social skills as an alibi for murder. But wait a second, he still lied to me!

"Wow, so you lied to me about everything this weekend. Even about the invite. You said *they* invited you." My forehead scrunches in anger. I hate being lied to.

"Sorry, honey. But I'm confident nobody is going to question any of us. Because I have a perfect plan. And now that you know about my plan, it's your turn to tell me the truth. What the hell were you planning to do after you shot Gia? What would happen if you *really* killed her?"

"Well, I didn't have an actual plan until I saw her gun case in her bag. Then I thought of yours, and that's why I was trying to look for it. I just knew I was going to kill her once you asked me to go on this trip. I didn't know how I was going to do it until I got here. Now that I think about it, guns are too loud. Unless the other people camping on the beach leave, then we can't use yours or hers. Not that we *would* be able to use hers unless I steal it when she isn't around—"

"—Honey," Jordan rests his hand on my thigh. "I'm really glad I took my gun out of the car this time. You realize whether you killed or injured her with it, you still would've ended up in prison. There's no way you could handle being locked up."

"Well, it's a good thing your gun wasn't in the car after all," I shrug.

Not having a strategy was not such a great idea, admittedly. But anger consumed me. All I knew was that I wanted Gia dead. I still love my husband. Regardless of if he cheated on me, I could never kill him. The image of stabbing him, suffocating him, and even setting him on fire did appear in my mind one too many times while I drank endless glasses of wine in New York. But even if he did cheat on me though, I could never bring myself to act on those thoughts. Gia, on the other hand, I was ready to kill her no matter how I was going to get it done.

"Now tell me, what is your well thought out plan to kill Levi? Elaborate on your strategy to get him to drown himself tomorrow night," I say.

"Well, it's not as simple as it sounds," Jordan says.

"Well, obviously killing a person isn't easy."

"You clearly thought it would be when you got here, Bonnie," he smirks as he brushes the side of my cheek.

"I love you, Clyde." I reach over the center console to kiss him. I can't believe I ever even doubted my husband's fidelity when we are actually the perfect couple. And we are quite in sync. We are the perfect couple who will kill a person together. Maybe this is what has been missing in our marriage after all these years.

1 0

Jordan

Gia and Richard think they were invited on this trip to celebrate Richard's birthday. Not because they need to be my alibi for when I murder Levi. As for my dimwitted insecure wife, she now unfortunately, knows why I really planned this trip.

Once I realized how serious Lily was about killing Gia when she thought Gia was my mistress, I knew telling her the truth about this trip was my only option. If not, we would have had two dead bodies on this beach instead of one and two dead bodies is not a part of my plan. I have no time to clean up Lily's mistakes this weekend.

If I hadn't showed Lily my meeting with Gia at the bar for Richard's surprise party, Lily would have still figured out a way to harm her or try to kill her. With or without my gun. That's why I caved and told her about my plan to kill Levi. Telling her the truth distracted her from harming an innocent woman. Gia does not deserve to die. Levi does.

Lily's desire to want to join me in killing Levi did not cross my mind though. Then again, she was ready to kill a woman under the false pretenses of an overheard conversation. And she didn't even have a proper strategy to get the job done either. My wife is impulsively ignorant most of the time. My only choice now is to include her in my plans this weekend.

Although Richard and Levi have complained about how far away from the bathrooms and airstream bar our tents are, I don't care because little do they know, I made a conscious decision to setup here.

This is a public beach but it is isolated enough that there aren't many people here. Thankfully, there are only three other families accompanying us on this little beach this weekend. I was hoping it would be just me, my wife, Richard, Gia, and Levi, but three other families are better than a packed beach so I'll take it.

Everyone else is well spread out from each other, especially away from us. Hence the reason I made sure me and Lily got here before Richard, Gia, and Levi did. I purposely set the tent up all the way at the end of the beach. Once they got here, camp was already set up so they had to set theirs up too. No time for any of the three of them objecting to my choice of location to pitch our tents.

The airstream bar opens at two in the afternoon and closes at eleven at night. So any time after eleven, it's just the campers. There is no need to worry about a lifeguard or any security roaming around out here.

There wasn't an area in the Keys that looked one hundred percent isolated that would keep us away from people where we could camp, so this beach had to do. I figured as long as we are far enough away from the parking lot and bathrooms, nobody else would come near us to pitch their own tents.

People are lazy. They don't want to walk an extra few minutes on the hot sand if they don't have the need to. Especially if they want to be close to their cars and of course, the bathroom. It takes about a good ten-minute walk to get to the parking lot from here. This is a perfect secluded spot to kill Levi without anybody seeing.

My plan: Get everybody drunk, especially Levi. He needs to black out after everyone else goes to bed. Then I will get him to walk along the water where he will eventually drown and drift off into the ocean to never be seen again.

First, I need to make sure Gia gets drunk enough that she'll want to go to bed early and Richard will have to go with her. When a woman says it's time for bed, normally the man follows. I'll make sure Richard will have plenty of drinks by then so they'll both fall right to sleep in their tent and I won't have to worry about them waking up. Knowing Levi, he'll want to stay up late and continue to drink with me. As for getting Gia drunk, that's where Lily will have to help me.

During our time here, I have only seen Gia drink martinis and margaritas from the airstream bar like Lily has. They haven't touched a beer or a shot of tequila from my cooler yet. Lily needs to befriend Gia enough to get her to want to keep drinking out of my cooler after the bar closes. My wife is not a social person and after hearing that she thought Gia was my mistress, I am not sure I can trust her with this task. Unfortunately, I have no other option. This is where her years of working in hospitality needs to be of use to me.

If all goes according to plan, once Richard and Gia go to sleep in their tent, Lily will go back to ours. And finally, it will just be me and Levi alone by the campfire. The cooler full of beer and tequila should be sufficient enough to get him blackout drunk.

Now it is time to tell Lily what her role is for tomorrow. Hopefully, she will actually listen to me and not object or make up her own suggestions.

"If Gia doesn't seem drunk enough to pass out, you need to talk her into drinking with you more. We need to make sure both her and Richard won't wake up throughout the night. I don't know how long it will take me to get Levi to go in the water after you all leave us alone to go to sleep. Make sure they stay in their tent and you can be my lookout while I'm with Levi. I'll convince him to go for a night swim or something and then I'll drown him."

"That's dangerous! He's going to struggle and end up fighting back!" Lily shrieks.

"He'll be too drunk to struggle, that's if he even tries to struggle at all. His motor functions won't work as well as when he is sober. I'll be able to get an advantage on him easily. Trust me."

"You have to leave your gun with me. I can use it if shit goes awry," Lily nods, eagerly.

"Honey, I'm not comfortable with you using my gun. I'll keep it on me." I fight the urge to laugh at her. I know she is trying to help, but I cannot trust my wife with a deadly weapon. My gun isn't even going to be with me when I drown Levi. It will stay in a bag next to the fire instead but she won't know that. Neither will Levi. I would love to shoot him and get the job done quickly, but the noise would give me away and point a finger right at me as the murderer.

"After I get Levi to go in the ocean, I'll drown him, then I'll come back to the tent, dry off and get in bed with you. In the morning, we'll wake up and we will all be shocked when we can't find him anywhere."

"What?" Lily shakes her head. "Honey! You can't just hope his body will drift off in the ocean," she argues. "If he doesn't turn up dead, then you can't cash in on any life insurance. You need definite proof that he's dead. Not just missing. You can't cash in on a life insurance policy if there is no dead body. He would just be categorized as a missing person."

Shit. How the hell did I not think of that? Of all things, how did I overlook that very important piece of my plan? Lily is right. Looks like I am slightly grateful my wife has become a part of my plan after all.

Now, how do I fix this?

"Damn, between the two of us, we're not really good at this murder thing." I can't help but make a joke. If Lily got her hands on my gun, someone would have been injured. Probably not dead because my wife can't shoot for shit. Then she would have spent her life in prison for attempted murder on an innocent person. And now look at me. I thought I had Levi's murder all figured out, but damn was I wrong.

"That's why we're better when we work together rather than by ourselves," she says with a deviant glossy eyed smile.

This is exciting to her. Murder excites my wife. Maybe I have misunderstood Lily all along.

"Instead of letting Levi drift off in the ocean, you need to bring him back on the sand and make it look like you tried to save him from drowning. Then call 9-1-1. Say you tried to resuscitate him. You have to make it appear like you tried hard to save him before he died."

"I can't be the number one suspect though," I say. "You're all supposed to be my alibi, but if I'm alone out there, then technically, I have no alibi. My plan was to let his body disappear in the ocean and then all of us would call the police and probably get questioned the next morning. I wasn't thinking about not being able to cash in on the insurance without a body."

"You won't be the number one suspect because I'll vouch that I saw him almost drown. I'll tell the police I saw it all from the tent— I went to use the bathroom and when I came back, I witnessed you pulling him out of the ocean, then giving him CPR. If Richard and Gia get questioned by the police, they'll say they were asleep because I'll make sure that they were, like you told me to do. Then I'll tell them the same thing that I'll tell the police, so they won't become suspicious. Not that I think they will, but just in case. This is perfect because spouses can't testify against each other in court so if anything, we're covered."

"I can't bring his body back after drowning him. What if an autopsy is ordered?"

Lily is smart and I am grateful that she brought up a good point. She is also fucking my plan up though. Now I'm unsure of how all this will go. I thought about the risk of an autopsy on his body because if it looks like a crime scene, one will surely be ordered. That's why I didn't want his body to be found. I wanted him to be reported missing.

"Nobody is going to ask for an autopsy on his body because he doesn't have anyone that will care enough about his death to ask for one. The police will only request one if they think his death is suspicious. A drowning makes perfect sense, especially when you tell them you tried to resuscitate him. It doesn't sound like that Sharon woman would care enough about him since you said he abused her. You told me he doesn't have any family either. You said he isn't close to his relatives and his parents are dead, right?"

"Right," I answer.

I did my research before strategizing how to kill Levi which is why I decided to do this. Nobody should care when he dies. That's for damn sure. So then, I guess Lily's idea will work. It has to because now she won't let me let his body drift off. I'll just drown Levi as I originally wanted to do, then pull his dead body back on the sand, attempt to resuscitate him with CPR, and make sure to fail. That way, the story we tell the cops will be mostly true. We'll just leave out the part of me drowning him. His death will look like a drowning on its own.

Tomorrow night can't come any sooner.

11

Islamorada,
Florida Keys.
Camping trip
Day 3

A heavy downpour rattles the tent, awakening me from a dead sleep at seven o'clock in the morning. The weather radar app on my phone indicates that the rain will continue for the next few hours, and will persist into tonight with periodic breaks in the rain every now and then.

Well, what a perfect day to plan a murder.

"These tents are fully waterproof right?" Lily mumbles as she awakens half-asleep.

My instinct is to respond with, *well are you getting wet?* Because all of our things in here including Lily herself, are obviously perfectly dry so her question is invalid. I refrain from my instinctive response to answer sarcastically though.

"We're fine," I tell her just when my phone starts to ring.

"Richard's calling," I sigh before answering and putting the call on speaker. "Hey, man."

"Looks like we're getting rained out this weekend. I checked the radar. It's gonna rain until tomorrow night. Everything's gonna get all wet out here. Mosquitos will eat us alive. Me and Gia are packing up and heading out in a little bit. At least we got two good nights in."

No. No. No. If they leave early, Levi will want to go with because he came with them in Richard's car. *Shit. Shit. Shit.* This is not how this weekend is supposed to go. They all need to stay here, especially Levi. Or else this trip was a waste of money, gas, and my time.

"Nah, let's not let the rain stop us. We can still have a good time. The tents are waterproof. We can drink and get hammered in the rain. So what if we can't make a fire? We'll still have—"

"—It's all right, man. No sense in camping when there's no campfire," Richard cuts me off. "Gia's prone to getting bit by mosquitoes anyways and she'll be miserable if we stay here. I'll see you in the office Monday. Thanks for this weekend. We had a good time."

Before I can convince him otherwise, the call ends.

"I got to call Levi and talk him into staying before Richard tells him they're leaving," I say to Lily while frantically scrolling over to Levi's name in my contacts.

"Morning, man," Levi answers. "Rain woke me up. It's pouring outside."

No shit.

"Yeah, it woke us up too. Richard and Gia are heading back home soon, but me and Lily are staying. I know you came with them, so you can head back with us."

"Ya'll really wanna stay out here in this rain? What's the point? We're just gonna be stuck in the tent."

"It's not gonna pour down on us all day. We'll get a few breaks in the rain and I got dry wood in my car. We can still have a campfire once the rain stops and there's still a cooler half-full of beer and tequila. We can go out and explore the beach even if we can't get a fire going. A little rain won't hurt us. What do you got to do at home anyway?"

Levi has nobody and nothing to go home to. Reminding him he has no life has got to convince him to stay here. He recently told me he's been staying in a motel since Sharon kicked him out of her apartment, so he doesn't even have a real home to go back to anyway.

"I guess you're right," Levi yawns. "I'm not really keen on running back to the motel. Oh, did I tell you? I'm moving into an efficiency on Monday. Getting the keys in the morning, then moving right in. So I probably won't make it into the office."

Oh, Levi. You're not even making it off this beach after tonight.

"That's great, man! Good for you. See, that's something we should celebrate tonight. A new future ahead for you."

Lily rolls her eyes as I shrug. *I'm trying really hard to get him to stay here, okay?*

"Okay, I'll see you when the rain lets up. Gonna down a few beers and enjoy the sound of the rain in here," Levi says.

Good. Start drinking early. Get your ass drunk already, so I won't have to do too much work when the time comes tonight.

"Honey, I thought you wanted Gia and Richard here when you kill Levi," Lily whispers once I end the call with him. The sound of the battering rain masks our voices from anyone hearing us outside though. There is absolutely no need to whisper in here.

"You heard Richard. He made up his mind. Couldn't really talk him out of it. Don't worry. You'll have to be my only witness now," I say.

Lily sits straight up. That deviant adrenaline filled smile is back. "Actually, this is even better. No need to worry about them waking up while you—*you know*. I'll be your only witness! And like I said, I can't testify against you in court if anything does go wrong."

"Okay, but nothing is going to go wrong." I can't emphasize this enough. My plan is thoroughly thought out— well, besides my initial idea to let Levi drift off into the ocean, (Thank you, Lily). Also, minus another hiccup; this damn weather which will possibly hold me back to set up the campfire tonight. Other than that, everything will still go smoothly.

Campfire or not, I will convince that son of a bitch to get in the ocean tonight one way or another.

1 2

Executing Jordan's plan

Whether rain or shine, Levi will die tonight. I wasn't going to try to convince Richard to stay on the beach any more than I did because I am not one to be pushy or confrontational. He already decided on leaving with Gia and I know that once a woman tells a man what she wants, the man must oblige. There was really no sense in trying to talk him out of their decision. Or should I say, Gia's decision because I am pretty sure if Gia was not here, Richard would have wanted to stay on the beach and camp in the rain with us.

Anyway, what's done is done. They have already left the beach and so now we move on. At least, I do not have to worry about counting on my wife to make a friend with a woman she originally thought I was fucking.

Good. More booze for Levi. Less stress headaches for me.

Although the rain was not in the forecast when I planned this trip, the change of weather actually did me a favor out here because all of the other campers left the beach already. Nobody came to open the airstream bar up either. I guess the owner kept it closed for the day because they probably assumed everyone would leave the beach. And they were mostly right. We are all completely alone out here now. It's just me, my wife, and Levi.

The rain finally let up about twenty minutes ago, leaving the sand sticky wet and the mosquitoes out to feast. I immediately ran out to the car to get the dry wood and got the fire going. The rain should start up again in about an hour and a half, according to the radar. This is my only window to get everything done.

While Levi tends to the fire, poking the logs to keep the flames going, I pour two shots of tequila. One for him and one for me. He's already tipsy since he has been downing beers since this morning, so getting him blackout drunk should not take too long.

"Richard shouldn't have left," Levi says as he takes the shot of tequila from me and shoots it back. "I think he should have stayed because it feels kind of cooler out here because of the rain. Not as hot as when we first got here. Makes for nicer vibes by the fire. Kind of feels like winter."

Yes, this makes for way better vibes— An empty beach. An ocean to drown in. No one around. Just us three. No witnesses to your upcoming death. Come to think of it, the sound of a gunshot wouldn't be heard by anyone after all...

But no. What am I thinking? A gunshot wound is evidence of murder. I can't use my gun. I'll only use it if Levi somehow manages to fight back. Then I'll have to devise a story about how I had to act in self-defense or something.

"Not drinking Lil'?" Levi asks her as I shoot the shot of tequila back. I guess this camping trip put Levi under the assumption that he is now on a nick name basis with my wife. Looks like she doesn't seem to mind.

"No thanks. I'm a wine type of woman. Jordan seemed to have forgotten that about me when he packed the cooler though." She shoots me a side glare.

Oh, little does she know, I did not forget that about her at all. I purposely did not pack any wine or mixers to make margaritas with the tequila because Lily is an annoying drunk. I did not want her to get drunk at all so when she helped herself to the bar the first day, I cut her off immediately. Thank God the bar didn't open today. There would be no way I could get through tonight if she were drunk by my side. She would end up interfering when I kill Levi by talking too much, extending her welcome by the campfire, or when the time would come, she would just get in my way.

One thing I do like about my wife is her personality, only when she is sober though. I never wanted Lily to get to know Richard and Levi because they are just my business partners. The three of us became friends when we met at the gym years ago— best friends as Lily thinks for some reason.

Even so, they don't need to become friends with my wife.

The snap of the tab prying open against Levi's beer can echoes the night air. Seven beers and one shot down so far. He is bordering the thin line between tipsy and drunk. Levi can normally outdrink me so I have to make it look like I'm drinking just as much as he is tonight. He thinks I'm on my seventh beer with him, but in reality, this is my third drink. Lily has been helping me pour out the contents of the beer cans into the fire and behind our backs when Levi isn't looking our way.

Time for a second round of shots.

"Whoa, man. Another shot already? Tryin' to get me real drunk tonight, huh?" Levi laughs while willingly taking the shot from me. He shoots it back with a smile.

"What's a campfire without tequila, am I right? This trip was supposed to celebrate Richard's thirty-sixth but since the pussy left, might as well have a few rounds for him." I hold up my drink and cheers.

I pour two more shots. No more after this for me. "Damn, isn't this view nice?" I gesture toward the crashing waves of the ocean.

And that was Lily's cue to leave us alone and go to bed now.

"Well, time for me to turn in boys. Enjoy the night, you two. The bed is calling me," Lily says through a fake yawn. "Don't get too drunk, honey." She reaches over to kiss me.

"Nice wife yousss got there," Levi slurs after Lily disappears inside our tent.

Ah yes, he's slurring his words already. This is good. Good. Good. Good.

"How long you two've been togetha'? Can't remember if you've told meh," he sips his beer like it's a baby bottle, swaying side to side.

"Sixteen years together. Married fifteen. Our anniversary was last month," I answer.

"Damn. That's long. Pussy ain't as good as it used to be. Am I right?"

Wrong. It's the personality and connection between us that isn't the same.

"Gets better with age actually."

God, I really can't wait to kill this guy.

"I ain't never having a wife," Levi shakes his head. "Don't want a bitch naggin' me for the rest my life. No offense."

Okay, it's time to finally get rid of this guy. I can't take any more of this piece of shit. I'm ready to reach over and strangle him right now. While I fake a wobble in my step to stand up straight, I gesture toward the ocean. (Got to act like I'm just as drunk as Levi is). Although he's so fucked up, he probably won't notice the difference in whether I'm sober or not.

"Gooootta take a piss," I say before stumbling toward the ocean.

Asking a man to go for a walk on the beach together is gay. But drawing him toward danger isn't.

"Oh shit!" I yell once I reach the edge of the crashing waves coming on shore. Today's stormy weather must have caused the current to be a little rougher now. The ocean looked a lot calmer yesterday. While pointing ahead at the waves, I turn and yell, "Levi, man! Get over here! I just seen a shark!"

"Nah, no way! Where?" he shouts as I watch him struggle to stand up straight. He fails the second he gets to his feet. He falls down on the sand at first before shifting his weight onto his knees, then to his feet to get back up. *Well fuck! Imagine if he fell forward into the flames instead of on the sand!* That would have been a cleaner way for him to go. His fall would have saved me effort, strength, and time. His death would have actually been a true accident if the fire engulfed him. If only I thought of that before. I could have pushed him right into the flames. Too late now.

After managing to stand back up, Levi stumbles toward me as he trips over his own feet along the way. Once he reaches me, he grips my shoulder to keep himself steady.

"I swear I seen the fin of a shark just now! It was over here." I shrug away from his grasp and take a few more steps into the ocean, knee deep.

"Where you goin' man? Tryna' become a shark's dinner, are ya?" Levi laughs as he fights to remain upright against the crashing waves that are smashing up on his shins.

"Ah, come on, man. Don't be a pussy!" I shout over the loudness of the waves. Men do not like to be challenged. Especially by other men and especially while they're drunk.

"You're the p—pussy," Levi scoffs, taking my bait and staggers ahead of me. I step back a bit as he wades forward. He's almost waist deep into the water now. The force of the waves pushes him back as he ventures deeper in the ocean.

All it takes is a few more steps—

And there he goes! Levi loses balance as a wave hits him, he falls backward, the ocean engulfs his entire body.

Now's my chance. No turning back.

As he struggles to emerge from the water, fighting against the waves, I rush toward him, and grab his shoulders tightly from behind. Then I push him back down under the cold ocean. His arms flail briefly against the waves as his instincts to survive take over.

But his attempt to fight back quickly ends as his inebriation takes over his fight or flight response. His arms turn limp and suddenly, he stops resisting beneath my grip. And finally, he remains underwater, completely unresponsive.

The waves fight to pull him away from me and I desperately want to let him go, but thanks to my wife, I can't allow him to float away into the abyss. Lily was unfortunately right. No dead body means there will be no money to claim. I need to make this look like a real accident. Like I tried to save his drunk ass.

I grab Levi underneath his arms, then just barely drag his soak and wet body onto the sand. This is harder than I imagined it was going to be. He is already a few pounds heavier than me and he benches—used to bench, I should say, a whole twenty pounds more than me. Dragging him while his clothes are soaked against these rough waves doubles his body weight. This was something that hadn't crossed my mind.

But finally, my strength does not defeat me. I push through the pain and drop his weighted body by my feet. I lean on my knees, breathless. No amount of strength training and cardio prepared me for dragging a wet dead body out of the ocean.

"You did it!"

"Honey!" I gasp, startled.

I nearly fell on top of Levi at the sound of my annoying wife's voice. She was supposed to stay in the tent. I specifically told her to stay away from us. This is what I mean when I say I can't trust my wife. She does not listen to anything. She is too impulsive for her own good. Being impulsive is not a good trait.

"Make sure he stopped breathing completely," she tells me. As if that wasn't what I planned to do.

"No kidding," I grunt. "Honey, you were supposed to stay in the tent until I was done."

"I was too anxious and technically, you are done," she shrugs.

There is no pulse when I rest my index and middle finger on Levi's neck. No pulse on his wrists either. I put my ear up against his chest. No heartbeat. I wave my hand under his nose. No breath. For good measure, I attempt CPR. I've never tried to resuscitate anyone before so it's not like I am good at it, but on the off chance I do it correctly, I'll just kill him again.

But no. CPR doesn't work, thank God.

Good. Now there is proof I really tried to save him. Not sure whether or not the coroners will prove attempted resuscitation happened or not. Just in case, I tried.

Exhaling deeply, I nod. "He's dead."

She smiles. "Okay, good. Now make the call. Make sure you act frantic."

PART 2

13

One week after
the camping trip

My plan would have gone off without a hitch if Levi's mother did not request an autopsy on his body. I was taken by surprise when a detective just called from an unrecognizable number. It's normally unlike me to answer a phone number that is unfamiliar, so I am not sure what came over me when I picked up the phone. Although if I never answered, the detective probably would have surprised me with an in-person visit at my doorstep instead. In retrospect, I guess it is better I took the phone call after all.

The detective did not directly say that my wife and I are suspects during our phone conversation just now. He just let me know about the autopsy and open investigation. Apparently, Levi's mother does not believe he drowned. The detective said he only called to notify me that I may need to answer questions about the night Levi died even though I already made a statement to the police when we were in Islamorada. The tone in his voice sounded like he was suspicious of me though. Or maybe that is my anxiety kicking in because I did not expect anyone to request an autopsy. Especially from a woman who is supposed to be dead.

Levi told me his parents died in a small plane crash while on vacation in the Bahamas years ago. He was an only child, no siblings. No extended family either. And I did not just blindly believe everything he told me. I did my research. There was no proof of anyone living in relation to him. Not even any aunts or uncles. Not even a long-time best friend. There was no evidence of any immediate family member or close friends on his social media which he rarely posted on. I googled his first and last name. Nobody came up in relation to Levi at all.

When Levi left the office to go help out a mover with one of our trucks one day, he left his phone on his desk. That's when I had the idea to look through his contacts and messages. I wanted to make sure nobody was in relation to him that I couldn't find online. The dumbass didn't use a password so it was like fate tempted me to look through his phone, especially when he left it sitting on his desk unsupervised. If the phone had been password protected, I wouldn't have found extra confirmation that I could kill him without the risk of anyone caring about him.

But it wasn't password protected, thankfully. Nobody was named dad, mom, sis, bro, uncle or aunt in his contacts on his phone. There were only text messages between Sharon, me, Richard, and a few spam texts. The man had no life besides going to the gym, fighting with Sharon, and managing our moving company with me and Richard. The only person who seemed close to him aside from us was Sharon, which is kind of sad but it also makes sense for a piece of shit like Levi.

No one ever stopped by to visit him at work. Not that our business is a place where people just walk in. Regardless, nobody ever came to see him. He never spoke to anyone on the phone, other than customers when he would book moving appointments. He only ever spoke to Sharon on his cell phone. He had friends in the gym from what I've seen over the years. Not many but a few. All of who have never interacted with him outside of the gym though. Some of those guys who we talk to and workout with; we don't even know their names.

Nobody was supposed to ask questions about Levi's death. No one was supposed to care enough about him to pay attention when he died, or went missing as I originally planned to happen. Except all of my research proved me wrong because it turns out his mother isn't dead. And to make matters worse, she cares about him!

I realize now, this woman must have just been metaphorically dead to Levi. That would explain why he told me his parents died on vacation. That's why there was no trace of his mother's existence anywhere on his social media or in his phone. As for why this woman never appeared in my online searches, that remains a mystery.

They must've had an estranged relationship. Therefore, Levi told people she was dead. Now that part makes sense. I wish I thought of that being a possibility before I killed him, but I thought my research into his family was enough. Too damn late now.

Up until the detective spoke to me, I figured the person who got notified about Levi's accidental drowning was Sharon, but she told me nobody called her. It turns out, she heard about his death from me instead. Assumingly, Levi's mother must have been the one to be notified by police, which is why she asked for an autopsy. But if she was such a shitty mother to Levi, enough to make her son want to tell people she died, why would she be his emergency contact? And most importantly, why did she care enough about him to ask questions about his death?

Maybe because she was not a bad mom after all and Levi was actually a problematic son. Levi was always dramatic, a loose cannon, and irrational at times, so that theory would make sense. I just wish I came to all these conclusions before killing the bastard.

None of that matters anymore though because the investigation is already open. Can't dwell on the past, so I must move forward. Time to prepare for an eventual interaction with the police. The detective called to tell me I *might* be questioned. Since he did not just show up at my door or subpoenaed me to go to the police station—that helps me hang onto a little bit of hope that I am not a suspect in Levi's death after all. Emphasis on a little bit.

"You said Levi's parents died years ago!" Lily exclaims in a panic, seconds after I get off the phone with the detective. Clearly, she was eavesdropping on my phone calls once again. Hasn't she learned from when she eavesdropped during mine and Gia's video call?

"That's what Levi told me! I swear. I told you I even looked for his immediate family online. Social media stalked him. Checked his phone. No sign of a mother anywhere. No father either. How could I know he was lying about her dying? You can even ask Richard! He told both of us his parents were dead."

While pacing our kitchen, I try not to show my anxiety. This is bad for me. This, I didn't count for. No time for dwelling though, I must remind myself. I just have to move forward and have faith that the autopsy will prove he died from drowning in the ocean while he was overly intoxicated.

Because he *did* drown and he *was* drunk.

"This is all your fault, Jordan. You barely fucking knew the guy before getting into business with him and he was obviously a liar. Are you sure he was actually abusing that woman? What was her name again? You said, Sharon?" Lily takes a long sip of her wine as she leans back against the counter.

"Honey, I'm positive he was abusing Sharon. I told you I saw her bruises and she even showed me a video that she discreetly took of Levi throwing plates and yelling at her in the kitchen."

"You didn't mention that video to me," Lily scowls. A long sip of wine following her comment.

"Does that matter right now?" I sigh. Leave it to my wife to bring up unnecessary statements at a time like this.

"Are you sure she wasn't lying though? You didn't actually *see* him hitting her in the video, did you?"

"Yes, I am sure she wasn't lying. Now stop questioning me." It is a struggle to keep my frustration to myself while gritting my teeth.

Another big gulp of wine slides down her throat. This is what I mean when I said Lily talks way too much and asks too many useless questions when she drinks. Speaking of drinking, time for a drink myself. Where did she hide the tequila bottle from me? When we came back from our trip, I looked for a new bottle and couldn't find it. I know she hid it because she doesn't like me drinking. Oh, but imagine if I hid the wine from her! She damn well would throw a fit!

"We shouldn't worry, right? The autopsy should come back as a drowning because that's what happened," she says. She sits down at the kitchen table and dramatically chugs the rest of her wine, emptying the glass.

Aha! Well, that didn't take long to find. My impulsive wife hid my tequila bottle behind the fancy dinnerware set that she never uses in the cabinet over the fridge.

"Technically he didn't drown on his own. I assisted," I say while pouring a shot in my favorite shot glass that Lily also did a bad job of hiding.

She exchanges a look of disapproval at my drink, but chooses to go for the wine bottle to refill her empty glass. "But there's no evidence of you *assisting*, right?" she asks, raising her eyebrows.

"There *shouldn't* be any."

For my sake, there better not be.

14

Mike

My big sister is a murderer! Or from what I just heard, it sounds like she is more of an accomplice to one— her shitty ass husband being the prime killer.

It does not surprise me that Jordan is a killer, but it is surprising that my sister is married to one and even worse, condones his actions. I thought she would be smarter than that. What dumbasses! The both of them!

"Hello! Anyone home?" I slam the front door shut behind me for dramatic effect. Their wedding picture falls off the wall beside the door. I don't bother to pick it up and rehang it. "It's me!" I shout.

Their sudden silence tells me they obviously didn't hear me unlock and open the front door minutes before announcing myself.

Of course they didn't hear me come in. They were too busy panicking about whoever Levi is—their fallen victim.

"Hey, sis." I walk into the kitchen to see both of them. Their expressions—stunned. Half a glass of wine in Lily's hand as she sits at the table, her eyes widened at my arrival. A vein pops out of Jordan's huge forehead. An empty shot glass and a bottle of tequila on the counter sits next to him as he leans against it, his fingers practically turning red from gripping the counter so tightly. "Brother-in-law." I smirk at him. He doesn't smile back.

It is obvious we have an unspoken hate for each other. Never liked his vibes from the day my sister introduced me to him and now I really don't like the man after hearing he is a murderer.

The last time I saw Lily and Jordan was a few weeks ago and I can't even remember our interaction because I was so drunk. My sister says I tried to steal her car with my buddy, Jamie while we were down here in Miami for a music festival, except I have no memory of that night. Neither does Jamie. For all I know, Lily is lying. I've never even tried to steal a car sober, let alone drunk. I only remember bits and pieces of the music festival, then waking up on my sister's couch the next morning, hungover. Jamie was passed out on the floor. I woke up to Lily looking down at me disapprovingly while her fuck ass husband stared me down like he was planning to kill me.

Well shit, maybe he actually was! Am I the next victim on his list? Or was I supposed to be his first victim before he killed whoever the hell Levi is?

"What the hell are you doing here? How did you get in? The door wasn't unlocked, was it?" Lily looks at me frantically, like a deer in the headlights. She's probably wondering how much I heard of their conversation; if I heard anything at all.

Oh, sis. I heard all I needed to hear.

"Well, what a warming welcome. I have a key. Did you forget you gave me this?" I wave her house key in the air. This is my first time letting myself in without knocking and man, did I pick the right time to do so!

"Oh. Yeah, I remember. It's just that you've never used it before. I forgot about it." Lily exchanges a side glance to Jordan.

"When did you give him a key?" Jordan asks her while keeping a devilish glare on me. The knives are only a few inches away from his hand placement. I wonder if he's thinking about turning around to grab one and then stabbing me to death.

"When mom died," Lily mutters. "I gave him a copy in case he needed it when we were at her funeral."

"Good thing you didn't use it when you tried taking her car," Jordan huffs. "I'm going upstairs." He takes off with the tequila bottle and shot glass, shaking his head. He's clearly disappointed in my sister for trusting me to enter their home whenever I want.

I kind of don't blame him for being mad at her. After all, Lily and I have been estranged up until recently. But in my defense, during the short amount of time this key has been in my possession, I have never once broken their trust. Except for the car incident that I am still unsure if that even happened or not. But that has nothing to do with owning a key to their house anyway.

"Why are you here?" Lily asks me again with an exasperated sigh.

"Came to say hello." I open their fridge, then grab a can of beer which I assume must be Jordan's and snap the tab open. Knowing the can belongs to him will make this beer even more tasty. But as I bring the can up to my lips, Lily snatches it away.

"No alcohol allowed for you in this house. Not after you tried to steal my car while you were shitfaced drunk the last time you were here."

"Whatever. I already apologized for whatever you think I did with your car."

"Not what I *think* you did. What I *saw* you do. You tried to hotwire my car and thankfully you were too loud and drunk to succeed and you failed miserably at it."

"I have no memory of doing that shit at all." I snatch the can back from her and chug the beer, crushing the can right after. "I'm in town for a flooring job this weekend. It's down in Homestead. Can I crash here for the night?"

"So that's why you're here. I knew you needed something." Lily takes a sip of her wine, her eyes hazy. She looks tipsy.

"Come on, let me stay the night. I'll be gone in the morning."

"Homestead is still almost an hour away from me though," says Lily.

"More like forty minutes," I retort.

"An hour with traffic."

"That's fine. I don't mind the drive. Staying here will save me money on a hotel. The stingy bastard that hired me won't pay for one."

"You should have discussed lodging with your client before agreeing to take the job," Lily tries to scold me.

"Yeah, yeah. I know. I'm a dumbass. The job is only for two days anyway. Tomorrow, I'll be done. I worked all day today. I'm tired. Please, just let me crash on the couch. I'll be gone tomorrow morning and I'll drive home right after the job."

"Fine. But next time, call and ask me first. The key is for emergencies, not to just barge your way in. Don't put the TV too loud tonight either and no more beer."

Lily grabs a grocery bag from under her sink, then pulls out the five-pack of beer (which was a six pack before I just chugged a can) from the fridge and places the cans in the bag. She leaves the kitchen, mumbling under her breath about what an annoyance I am with the bag in her hand. On her way toward the stairs, she stops at the front door to rehang her wedding picture—the wedding I wasn't invited to. But to be fair, we weren't speaking back then so I'll let my forgotten invitation slide.

"So you think I'm an alcoholic now?" I shout as she disappears up the stairs. Although, I'm not even offended.

Oh, my sister has no idea what she's got coming for her. After I am finished with my job tomorrow, I'll make sure to let Lily know about how much I heard of her and Jordan's conversation. Soon, she will realize they are both going to be sorry for treating me the way they do.

15

An uninvited visit from mom

This is not a good time for a surprise visit from my mother. She knows me and Lily are going to work soon, so why come inconvenience us now, first thing in the morning? A cup of coffee and a hot shower are calling my name. In that order.

But instead, I am at my front door greeting my mother at eight o'clock in the morning, half-asleep. "Morning, mom."

At least she has the decency to knock before barging her way in though. Then again, that's because she doesn't own a key to our house. My own mother who lives a few blocks over doesn't have a key, yet Lily's conniving brother does. Why the hell would Lily think Mike deserves one? Yes, he's blood but he can't be trusted. He proved that when he tried stealing Lily's car in the dead of night.

"Good morning, son." My mom walks right by me and heads straight to the dining table. "Have you made coffee yet?" She eyes the empty coffee pot in the kitchen, knowing the answer.

"No. This is my first time coming downstairs this morning. Your knock and the notification on my phone from my front door camera woke me up. But I'll make some coffee now that you're here, mom," I groan while closing the front door. If only Lily and I were paying attention to our phones last night and heard the camera notify us of movement outside, then we wouldn't have been shocked when Mike let himself in.

Thud. And there goes our wedding picture. Our black and white memory encased in five hundred and seven dollars worth of a blackwood antique heavy frame falls on the floor. Lily just had to buy that damn thing after she made us book a photoshoot once we got married. I saw the picture on the ground last night before I went to bed. Lily must've hung it back up before she came upstairs. She's asked me to replace the nail in the wall for weeks now. I should do it soon before she throws more of a fit about it falling.

"You still haven't put a new nail up, son? That nail has been loose for weeks now. This is a beautiful photo of you two. You shouldn't allow it to keep falling on the floor. The frame is going to break."

Apparently, I should fix it before my mother throws a fit too. *Women.*

A downfall of living three blocks away from a parent is the delusion of said parent thinking they can come over at any given time, without a call or warning. That would be the main reason I can't trust my mother with a key to my house. Or else I'd end up waking up to see her making her own coffee instead of a knock on my front door.

"How are you doing?" she asks while I begin brewing the coffee.

"Tired," I answer.

"No. No." She shakes her head. "I'm talking about your work partner, Levi. How are you holding up? I heard he died during your camping trip."

"What?" I nearly drop the coffee pot. "How did you know he died?"

"I called Lily yesterday after I called your phone because you didn't answer. She told me you were talking to a detective. I wanted to know why because that worried me, so she told me about what happened on your camping trip. She told me Levi drowned." My mother lowers her voice and raises her eyebrows. "Is that true, son?"

Dammit Lily! I could strangle her! She not only trusts her idiotic little brother with a key to enter our home, she also told my mother information she does not need to know. Lily cannot keep her mouth shut, I swear. I underestimated her capability to keep Levi's murder a secret.

"Yes, sadly he did drown." I hand a cup of hot coffee to my mother. "I don't want to talk about it."

The look on her face indicates my words are unbelievable.

"Jordan, you need to tell me the truth. Did you have something to do with Levi's death?"

"What? Why would you think that?" I whisper.

Her silence tells all. It is obvious why she thinks that. Still, she shouldn't ask me that.

"Mom, just because I got rid of your boyfriend when I was barely an adult, doesn't mean I turned into a killer. Why would you think I killed Levi?"

"Because you were there when he died. All alone. Lily told me you were out drinking by the campfire with him when he went off in the water and drowned."

What the fuck! Lily promised she would be my alibi and say she watched me try to *save* Levi. She couldn't even remember to keep that lie going with my mother. She is supposed to tell everyone the same story. Not only to the police which she did follow through on the beach when they arrived, but still! How could she be so ignorant?! Oh, how I can't wait to have a talk with her later.

"Son, you can tell me the truth. I've kept your secret for over twenty years now. If you… if you got rid of Levi, I'm sure you had a good reason, right? I just want to make sure you're doing okay. Ever since that first time… when you got rid of my ex, I've always worried about you. Worried that I didn't handle that night properly. I don't want you to turn into a killer."

"Mom, I'm not turning into anything! That one time was the *only* time," I say, correcting her. "I had to protect you that night. Please, don't worry about me. I'm fine. What happened with your ex was an entirely different situation than what happened with

Levi. He got drunk and drowned. I tried to save him and I failed. End of story."

"You didn't fail, son. You tried and didn't succeed."

"That's the same thing, mom."

"Okay, well I just wanted to come here to check on you and let you know I'm here if you want to talk. Are you going to work today? It's awfully soon to go back since... since your partner passed."

"I own the place. Doesn't matter how soon it is," I sigh.

"You should take the day off to grieve him."

"Mom! I have to get ready for work. I haven't even showered yet. I hate to kick you out but..."

"Okay, okay. I understand. Call me if you need anything." She gets up from the table with my coffee cup in her hand. I don't bother to ask her to leave it here. She'll just add it to her collection of cups she has taken from me over the years.

As she passes the stairs and approaches the front door, she shouts, "Good morning, Lily! Your husband's kicking me out. He said, he's going to replace the nail for your beautiful photo soon. Love you! I'll see you later!"

"Nice one," I mumble as my mother shoots me a devious glare.

"Love you!" Lily shouts from somewhere in our bedroom above the stairs.

And like clockwork, the picture falls the moment my mother walks out and shuts the front door.

My mother is the only person who knows about what I have done in the past and it will stay that way. Given my history, it is fair that she only showed up to check on me after she heard how Levi died (thanks Lily). It is a little upsetting that my own mother believes I've turned into a killer because of the one time I defended her, but she cannot and won't know the truth about Levi. My past does not define me. Levi's murder was different. That does not make me a killer.

As far as my mother knows, I have only ever killed one person.

1 6

M i k e

Man, I really did pick the perfect time to show up unannounced and spend the night here! Jordan is such a fucking idiot. He admitted to murdering a different person while I am still in the house only a few feet away from him. He must not realize I am in the bathroom downstairs right outside of the kitchen where he was just whispering with his mother. Or he does know I'm still here and like I said, he is just an idiot.

I need to figure out who the hell else that jackass killed besides Levi. Who did he get rid of when he was *barely an adult*?

Barely an adult sounds like he was anywhere between eighteen or twenty years old whenever he killed whoever they were talking about. I can also assume *getting rid* of a person means he killed someone.

The fucker has killed two people!

And his mother knows about the first victim. He obviously lied to her about Levi being his second victim though. She sounded unconvinced that her son is not responsible for Levi's death and from what I heard of Jordan and Lily's conversation yesterday, she should be. What did his mother mean when she said she didn't handle that night well twenty-years ago? Her words implied she is worried he turned into a killer and from my understanding, again she should be. The woman's motherly instincts are stronger than she knows.

I wonder if my sister knows about her husband's first victim. Jordan and his mom were both whispering during their conversation, so I assume that was because they didn't want Lily to hear them. Unless they were keeping their voices low because he knows I'm in the bathroom and didn't want *me* to hear them. If so, they did a shitty job at trying to remain quiet.

Hopefully Lily doesn't know anything about Jordan's first victim because this new fact will give me more ammunition for when I have a conversation with her without Jordan around. Just me and her. I should leave the bathroom before Jordan figures out that I was eavesdropping... but too late.

The bathroom door suddenly swings open. Jordan stands on the other side, forehead creased. "Oh! What the fuck?" he huffs. His nostrils flared, that vein protruding in the middle of his big ass forehead. In the midst of eavesdropping on his conversation, I forgot I already unlocked the door because I was about to leave the bathroom. His conversation stopped me from departing. "Why the fuck are you here?" Jordan asks, his tone accusatory.

"Do you and my sister communicate at all?" I laugh. *Is that what marriage is all about— miscommunication?*

Jordan's pulverizing silent stare answers my question.

"I slept on your couch last night. I assumed Lily told you but it is obvious she didn't. I got a flooring job in Homestead today and needed to sleep somewhere."

"Are you staying tonight too?" he grunts.

"Nope. Don't worry. I ain't coming back. Just needed a place to sleep last night. That's all."

Jordan looks me up and down. "Are you done with the bathroom?"

"Don't you have your own bathroom upstairs?"

"Lily's using it. Are you done in here or not?" he repeats.

Smiling, I nod. "I was just leaving. No more hot water if you needed a shower though." I pat him on his back as I walk by him and head into the kitchen to grab my thermos of water out of the fridge.

On my way to the front door, I say, "Tell my sis I said thanks for letting me sleep here last night! Have a good day brother-in-law."

1 7

Twenty-two years ago, I was faced with a decision. To kill a man or continue to allow him to keep hitting my mother. There was no time for thinking. No time for planning. I acted on complete rage and an alcohol induced state as a young man.

At eighteen years old—I was only six months into being a legal adult the night I came home from a party and witnessed my mother fighting with her boyfriend once again. The guy was a skinny fuck who didn't see me coming. Once I saw his hands on her, everything went dark. I had no idea what I had done until I saw him bleeding out on the floor and my mother staring at me in silence. That's when my hands came into view, covered in red, bruised knuckles, and aching palms. Then I realized I was the reason for all the blood on me—*all his blood.*

I blame my father for that night. Although he had been long out of the picture before then, he is the reason for all the pain my mother endured. He abused her for as long as I can remember until they divorced when I was fifteen—the last time I saw and ever heard from the asshole. He was the first to lay hands on her. The first to start a trend my mother didn't know how to stay away from.

Following the divorce with my dad, my mom dated three guys. Each one of them either mentally or physically harmed her. Her third boyfriend only stopped hitting her because I beat him to death, literally. I never caught the first two guys laying hands on her, although it was apparent she had been in one too many fights with them because of all the marks on her face and arms.

You could say my mother attracted a type; that's for sure. But still, the blame for those idiots' abusive actions to a woman does not fall on her.

That's why when Sharon showed me what Levi did to her and her daughter, I came up with the perfect plan to cease Levi's existence. He needed to die. A man should never lay hands on a woman in an unhealthy and hurtful way. If they do, then they are not a man. They're a little pathetic boy, no matter what age they are.

When I caught my mother's shitty boyfriend hitting her, there was no time to think my actions through. I acted on complete defense. My alcohol induced state aided in my decision to attack the skinny fuck and it just so happened, I attacked him so hard, I literally beat the guy to death.

Killing Levi came under different circumstances than when I murdered my mother's boyfriend. Unlike the first time I got rid of a useless piece of shit, I had more time to strategize Levi's murder.

Everything went according to plan (except for my wife getting in the way and talking me into believing I had to bring Levi's body on the beach to prove he died to get my money) and until Levi's mother suddenly rose from the grave.

Women. I care for them so much, I kill others to protect them and yet they still find ways to get in my way. The nerve of these females!

The autopsy request is already in progress so finding Levi's mother and getting rid of her won't do me any good. Although I vowed to never get rid of a woman, no matter the circumstance, the thought has crossed my mind—Levi's mother could be an exception.

My conscience knows that will not look good during an investigation though. I just have to wait patiently and get through the police questioning, if that even happens, (lets pray it doesn't), and wait for the autopsy report to prove that Levi drowned. Because he *did* drown.

Once the investigation gets dropped, I can file a claim with the life insurance company without raising any red flags, pay off my debt, and live the rest of my life in peace. All this stress will be worth it in the end. I didn't kill another person for no reason. Everything will work out for me because if it doesn't, my vow to spare women won't survive much longer.

1 8

Knock. Knock. Knock. It's eight o'clock in the morning on a Friday. It's like the police knew that showing up in the morning right before Lily and I head off to work would be the perfect time to ruin my day. This time, I wish it were my mother on the other side of my front door instead of them.

A detective had only called me two days ago to *'inform me'* which let's face it—was more of a warning and a scare tactic, about the open investigation into Levi's death. I knew getting questioned by them would be inevitable after that call. I just didn't expect it to happen this fast, only two days later.

"H—honey?" Lily's voice trembles as she peers out of the window next to the front door. "It's two—"

"—Yes, I know. Go upstairs. Don't come down until they leave," I tell her. I don't have to look out the window to see who is there because by the loud and intimidating knock on my door, it's obvious there must be two police officers out there.

Lily kisses me before rushing up the stairs, eyes glazed with worry. Thank God she never got her hands on my gun and shot Gia.

She would do no good in prison or under questioning of a police officer. She is in no state of mind right now if she were to be questioned about Levi which is why I told her to stay upstairs. And she better listen to me. I will just tell them she is not home if they ask to speak with her.

Okay, here I go. With a sharp inhale and exhale, I open the door.

Well, shit. These are not police officers in front of me. They're *detectives*. Two men in plainclothes, sporting detective badges attached to their waistbands. Why is their presence much more intimidating than an officer in uniform? I should have expected to see detectives instead of the police since Levi's death is under an investigation. And after all, a detective *did* call me. All of this is becoming too real too fast.

Focus. Breathe. I can get through this. I got through this before. I can do it again.

"Hello? Can I help you?" I ask, hoping my anxiety cannot be heard in my tone of voice.

"Mr. Hoffman. I'm Detective Williamsburg and this is my partner, Detective Jameson. I spoke to you over the phone the other day. We have a couple of questions about your camping trip in the Keys last weekend. Levi Moore was your business partner, correct?" The shorter detective out of the two speaks first. For some reason, I expected the taller one to take the lead.

"Yes, sir," I nod.

"May we come in?" Detective Shorty glances over my shoulder.

"Uh, yeah." I clear my throat as I open the door wider. I was hoping to just answer their questions on my doorstep, but not allowing them in my house will make me look suspicious. "Come on in."

After they walk in and the door shuts behind them, that damn wedding picture falls on the floor. The reminder of the loose nail I have not bothered to replace, despite Lily and my mother's endless reminders nag at me. Replacing a nail is the last thing on my mind right now.

"Gorgeous photo," Detective Shorty nods as I pick up the ten-pound frame—a reminder of my wife's unnecessary expense. I hang it back on the loose nail, knowing it will most likely fall again when these guys leave.

"Thank you." I lead them to the living room, only a few steps away from the door. No need for them to go any farther into my home. Let's make this quick and snappy. "Please, make yourself comfortable." I gesture toward my couch for them to take a seat. I think twice about offering them a cold beverage. No need to make myself look like an overachiever or an over compensator. Let's just get straight to the point.

"Sir, if you could please go over the events of the night before you called 9-1-1 when you found Levi unconscious on the beach?"

"Certainly. After my wife went to go to bed in our tent, I stayed up to drink a few more beers with Levi by the campfire. Levi drank a little bit more than me which was normal. He liked his beer."

"So it was just you two on the beach? Any other campers nearby?" Detective Shorty interrupts me.

"Only us. No other campers. Everyone left that day because of the rain. My—"

"—Including your other business partner, Richard Stallman and his fiancé. They left early too, correct?" Detective Shorty interrupts again. He's got an angle and he's building up to it.

"Correct. They both left earlier that morning. I think it was around nine or ten o'clock."

"In the statement your wife gave to the officer on scene, she said she witnessed you trying to resuscitate Levi. But you just said she went to bed and left you two alone, sir. How did she see you when she was asleep?" Detective shorty asks, his tone accusatory.

I'm prepared for this. Play it cool. Reiterate exactly what I rehearsed and said to the officers on the beach.

"Well, she did go back to our tent with the intention to fall asleep until she came out a few minutes later to walk to the bathrooms. That's when she saw me trying to help Levi out of the water."

Fuck. Detective Shorty sounds like he has plans to question her next. That cannot happen. Lily isn't strong enough for an interrogation.

"Okay, so let's back track. Tell me what happened before Levi ended up in the water." Detective Shorty's angle is to confuse me. I see it now.

Does the other detective whose name I already forgotten, even speak at all or is he just here to look pretty? Whatever he said his name was, he is now Detective Mute to me.

"Well, me and Levi sat by the fire, maybe for about ten minutes or so before he went to go take a piss in the ocean. I was scrolling on my phone, realized how late it was, so I decided to get ready to put the fire out. I went to grab the bucket of water we were keeping by the picnic table and that's when I noticed Levi was deeper in the water than he should have been—from his neck up only. His arms were kind of... flailing in the air and I knew something was wrong," I sigh to emphasize how traumatizing of a night it was.

"It was obvious he was struggling. So then I ran over to him and when I got closer, Levi was gasping for air. I jumped in, grabbed him, and pulled him out of the water. When I pulled him back on the sand, that's when I realized he wasn't moving and he stopped gasping. Wasn't speaking or anything. I tried resuscitating him, but sir... I-I never conducted CPR on anyone until that night and like I said, I had a few beers in me, so I admit I wasn't sober, but I wasn't drunk enough to not know what I was doing either. If that makes sense, sir."

"You were a bit more than buzzed." Detective Mute finally speaks up. Turns out he does know how to talk after all.

"So, you didn't initially see Levi actually go in the water, right?" Detective Shorty takes over again.

"No. I saw him walk toward the ocean but I did not see the moment he got in. I'm guessing he stumbled in a little drunk or I don't know what happened, really. He told me he went to take a piss, like I said. I was scrolling on my phone, then I turned to pick up the bucket of water to put the fire out and that's when I caught a glimpse of Levi in the water. The waves were up to his neck. It almost looked like the tide was trying to take him. The waves were a bit rough from the storms earlier that day."

The detectives exchange subtle glances. Detective Shorty takes the lead again. "How did you pull Levi out of the water? I imagine it was probably difficult to pull him out against the waves with the ocean weighing him down while you were intoxicated."

"Oh, yes sir. It was a bit of a struggle but honestly, the events of that night are kind of blurry. I did struggle to save him but sir, I wasn't drunk. Like your partner said, I was buzzed. And once I saw him struggling, my adrenaline sobered me up really quick."

"Mr. Hoffman, would you mind demonstrating on my partner here, how you pulled Levi out of the water?" Detective Shorty's request almost makes me lose my composure.

This was unexpected. I just explained the entire night and now he wants a demonstration? Is that even legal? He's treating me like a suspect! I should ask for a lawyer but that would make me look guilty. I've already made it this far into questioning without a lawyer anyway. And then, if I do ask for one, I'll have to explain to the lawyer the same lie I am telling these detectives. *Fuck my life.*

Nodding, I stand up. "Sure. No problem."

Detective Mute gets up from the chair and drops to his knees in an awkward position in front of me. I guess since I said Levi's head was basically bobbling out of the water, this is the best way to mimic the situation. He begins to fling his arms in the air which looks ridiculous and slightly humorous. But laughing at him would be unwise of me in this situation. I scratch my head while thinking about how to do this.

"Well, we were in the water. The waves were making it a bit hard to grab hold of him like you said, sir and it's kind of hard to recreate what happened here," I gesture toward his animated partner who seems like he missed his calling to be a mime.

"Do your best," Detective Shorty says.

Awkwardly, I slightly bend my knees to grab hold of the detective's waist, making sure to reach around from behind him and not the front. His body falls limp in my arms and we drop down on the ground as he falls on top of me. While struggling, I move onto my knees to stand up and shift backward so I can drag him against the carpet. As if I were dragging him across the sand like I did with Levi.

"So you grabbed Levi from behind. Not from the front of his body?" Detective Shorty asks as he watches me closely.

"Correct," I nod, motioning to my very awkward and a bit inappropriate position with Detective Mute in my grip. "Just like this."

"And did you place your hands anywhere else on him?"

"Not that I can remember. Everything happened so fast. I just wanted to make sure he was okay."

"Interesting." Detective Mute makes himself comfortable on my couch again. "The coroners found marks on Levi's body."

Shit. Shit. Shit. What marks? Did I bruise him when I pushed him down in the water? I don't think my grip was strong enough to leave a mark on his shoulders. He only struggled for a moment. Not even long enough for me to fight him. The waves helped me keep him down under the water, especially under his drunken state of mind.

This was a mistake. I should have asked for a lawyer before reenacting what I supposedly did with Levi in front of these detectives. I did pull Levi out of the water in the way I just explained. These detectives just don't know that I pushed him down beforehand.

Or do they? Is that why he just mentioned the marks? Or maybe there aren't any and he's trying to call my bluff.

"Oh... from when I pulled him out of the water, you mean? Like I said, he was a heavy guy. I was frantic. I didn't mean to leave marks on him. I just really wanted to get him out of there... I wish... I wish I did the CPR correctly. I could have saved him." I drop my head in an effort to show my desolation.

"At least you tried your best to rescue him, Mr. Hoffman," Detective Shorty says. "Is your wife home? We'd like to speak with her for a minute."

"No, she's at work."

"Whose car is outside then? I saw two vehicles in your driveway." Detective Mute speaks up.

"Oh, that's because my mother took my wife to work today. Mine and Lily's cars are outside. She just doesn't like driving often so my mother offers to drop her off and pick her up. She only lives a few blocks over."

They better not try to talk to my mom and corroborate that. Fuck. Fuck. Fuck. Why did I just say that?

I thought getting rid of Levi would go smoother than this, but now things are falling apart. They're falling apart fast.

"No problem. We'll swing by another day to talk to your wife," Detective Shorty stands up. Detective Mute follows him.

"Sure. Let me know if there's anything else you need from me."

After I walk them out of my house, I lock the top and the bottom locks on the front door with trembling hands. Our wedding picture falls off the wall and down comes Lily from the stairs.

"Honey, is everything okay? I heard the whole conversation. I could have talked to them," she says.

"No. No. No. You are not talking to them." I head toward the kitchen to get far away from the front door. Just in case the dimwits are still lingering outside the house.

Mimicking my interaction with Levi was not in my plan. When I got rid of my mother's boyfriend, two police officers questioned me on the scene, but not in the way those detectives just spoke to me. My mother and I told the officers her boyfriend fell and hit his head because that's where all my punches landed. We said he was so drunk, he fell and they believed us.

But this time, I was asked to demonstrate what happened. Demonstrate! I was being treated like a suspect!

"This isn't good," I mumble.

"Jordan, calm down." Lily follows me to the kitchen.

"Lily, did you not hear what they just made me do? I'm a suspect! This wasn't supposed to happen. And why the hell did you tell my mom about Levi?"

"Because she asked where you were and I wasn't thinking when I said you were talking to a detective on the phone," she shouts.

"Exactly. You never think!" I yell while making a pot of coffee.

"Don't yell at me!" Ironically, she yells at me to not yell at her. *Hypocrite.*

"There isn't any evidence that you killed him, honey," Lily lowers her voice. "We're fine. You're fine. Everything is going to be okay. We just need to be patient. Once the autopsy results come back, we won't have to worry about anything, right? It should just show that he drowned. That's it. Right?"

For her sake, I hope she's right because if the police charge me with Levi's murder, it might not be long before they charge me with another.

19

Is Richard going to be a problem now?

Richard took a few days off work after I broke the news to him about Levi. He couldn't handle coming in so I told him not to sweat it. I said I would take care of the business while he stayed home to grieve. But now, he's back and he is staring at me from his desk, oddly.

Is he thinking about our camping trip last weekend? Is he wondering what truly happened to Levi after he left me alone with him? Does he believe the drunk drowned on his own? Does he miss the lying bastard at all? And does he know the cops came to my house this morning? Should I ask if they went to his?

He's giving me a strange uncomfortable look, like he is contemplating something... as if he's suspicious of something. Suspicious of me?

Is he going to be a problem now?

Or am I being paranoid?

Yes, I'm being paranoid. I need to cut this shit out and remain confident. The detectives spooked me this morning. That's why I am questioning everything right now, that's all.

I have never seen Richard look at me like this though. I should say something. Break the silence. This is getting awkward.

"What's up, man?" I ask as casually as possible.

"How are you doing?" Richard sips his coffee, eyebrows furrowed.

"Um, I'm fine. How are you?"

"You sure you're alright? I mean, I can't see how you're just... doing fine. You tried to rescue Levi and you're just... kind of acting like nothing happened. Aren't you traumatized? You didn't need to come in today. I appreciate you holding the place down the past few days while I was gone but you could've stayed home today. I feel like an asshole for not coming in and letting you take over. You were the one who should have stayed home instead."

"Oh, don't worry. It's no problem, man. Of course that night was traumatizing, but I'm better off here. Got to keep going. Can't sit at home and sob all day. No offense. I just, I grieve differently than you do."

"Right. I get it." Richard stares at me. "I still feel guilty I wasn't there when it happened. I wish I didn't leave the beach early."

"Don't be, man. Shit happens," I shrug.

"Right. Shit happens... I guess," he says, but he is still looking at me skeptically. Time to ramp up my emotions.

"Okay. Actually, you're right," I exasperatedly sigh. "I'm not *fine*. I just don't want to be home. If I stay home, I'll think about what happened. Shit was intense, man. The moment I saw him panicking in the water, reaching for help—when I grabbed him and tried to resuscitate him. Shit, the whole night is all a blur, but at the same time, it isn't. I just know I tried to save him from drowning and I failed. I need to be here in the office because work distracts me. I know that sounds insane since this is the one place that should remind me of him, but still, I just feel better when I'm here."

"This place keeps you busy. I get it. Don't be so hard on yourself though. You can't blame yourself for what happened. Shit sucks. Did you know his mom asked for an autopsy?"

"I heard," I nod while fighting the urge to roll my eyes. *That risen from the dead bitch. If I did not vow to keep my hands off a woman, she'd end up my next victim, I swear.*

"I guess that means there's an investigation open because a couple of detectives came to ask me questions this morning. They caught me when I was backing out of the driveway," Richard says.

"Oh, really?" *Shit*. I did not want to hear that. Why would those detectives have an interest in speaking with Richard when he wasn't even at the scene? I assume they stopped at his house after they stopped at mine because he got to the office two hours after me this morning. They probably went to corroborate our stories after speaking with me. *Fuck.*

"Yeah. You know, I swear Levi told me his parents were dead. I could be wrong, but didn't he tell you that too?" Richard asks.

"Yeah, he did tell me that. Guess he lied to us." *And we stupidly believed him.*

"Maybe he was joking when he said it. You know how he could be," Richard shrugs.

"Not sure, man. So, what did the detectives want from you?" I ask while keeping my tone as nonchalant as possible.

"They wanted to know what time me and Gia left the beach and if there were any fights between you two."

"Me and Levi?"

"Yeah. I thought that was a weird question to ask me. I told them that there weren't problems between any of us. They seemed satisfied with my response. I mean, I was telling the truth. It's not like you had anything to do with how he died. Hell, you tried to rescue him. I don't understand why his mom requested an autopsy. Makes no sense. It was clearly an accident how he died."

"True," I say. "The detectives talked to me this morning, too. They wanted me to explain how I pulled him out of the water. Man, you have no idea how that felt. Having to relive that night was wild. It's hard not to blame myself because I could have saved him if I just got to him a few seconds sooner. I knew he was drunk but I didn't think anything of it when he went to take a piss. I don't even see how he got dragged in by the water. The waves weren't too rough."

"That's if he got dragged in. You said he was drunk. He probably went in on purpose," Richard suggests. "No one ever makes smart decisions when they're drunk, especially Levi. If only he walked to the bathrooms instead but hell, I would've done the same thing—gone in the ocean. But we can't harp on what happened. We just got to keep his memory alive here. Without him, we wouldn't have been able to even start this place up."

That is true. Levi was the first person to sink his own money into this business before the three of us got approved for a few business loans. Between Levi's money and the loans, we were all able to get this place up and running quite quickly. But in hindsight, if Richard and I wanted to start the business without Levi, I'm sure we could have done it easily. It just would have taken more loans, limitations, and time. Richard originally came up with the idea to open a moving company in the first place. Levi was all for it and invested his savings right away. He came up with the name, SoFlo Miami Movers too.

Well fuck my life again. How did I forget about that? Hopefully, Levi's initial role in our business does not constitute an investigation against me. That is, if there isn't one already. After my interaction with the detectives this morning, I am not sure what to think about all this.

What I can do is blame Lily for all of this though. All this happened to save innocent Gia from potentially getting shot by my insecure and dimwitted wife. If Lily hadn't accused me of anything, she would have stayed out of my plan.

See what I mean? Women! They even get in my way when I go to great lengths to protect them. Especially Lily. I not only protected Gia from my wife; I protected my own wife from herself too. If I allowed her to get her hands on my gun, Lily would have ended up in prison, regardless of how and who she used it on. Now look at where all that *protecting* has got me—in constant stress and under investigation.

If only I allowed Levi to drift off in the ocean. No body, no crime. Surely, I would have gotten the payout from the insurance company somehow, someway. Maybe it would've taken longer to process, but what the hell? It's taking longer than I planned now with the investigation open. I haven't even been able to file the damn claim yet!

This is all wrong. I love Lily and I also cannot stand her. She never thinks anything through and I have to withstand the brunt of it all; hence her plan to shoot poor innocent Gia. If I did not show her the evidence of planning a birthday get-together for Richard, I would have had to clean up my wife's mess, along with dealing with all this shit.

In a way, mine and Lily's mindsets alike show how much we can be perfect for each other—killing excites us. Even after over a decade of marriage. Even though she gets on my nerves. Even though there are times when I've questioned how much in love we still are.

And yet, at times, among her many annoying tendencies, my wife tests my patience to fight the urge to strangle her.

2 0

M i k e

Lily thought I left town the other day, but that was a lie. Oh, the perks of working as an independent contractor. I can take a job as needed and not be on a nine to five schedule. My flooring job down in Homestead ended two days ago and I planned on going back home to Jacksonville afterward until I learned about Jordan's serial killing side hobby. That's when I decided I couldn't go home just yet.

So, I booked a cheap hotel in the area, just so I can stay in Miami, and catch my sister off guard— right here in the parking lot of her own job. It's five o'clock in the afternoon. This is a perfect time to bombard her because she just got out of work. She's tired, stressed, and more than likely, she probably just wants to get home to her murderous husband. She won't have any energy to argue with me, so this is the perfect moment.

"What are you doing here?" Lily groans when she sees me leaning against the hood of my truck in the parking lot.

"I love how excited you are to always see your one and only little brother," I smile.

"Mike," she sighs. "What do you want? What's going on?"

"I came to chat about your conversation with your husband."

"What the hell are you talking about? What conversation?"

Grinning, I say, "I heard everything the other day. I know Jordan drowned Levi and you were there when it happened. Don't lie to me because I heard you guys talking about it in the kitchen when I let myself in the other night."

"Shh!" She grabs my arm and yanks me closer to my driver's side door. Don't know what good that did because we are still standing in a parking lot full of cars if she doesn't want anybody to hear us. Tons of people are walking in and out of the diner. Most of them are heading to the vehicles parked only a few spots near us.

"W—what are you talking about?" she whispers.

"Did you not just hear me? The other night when I slept over. Remember when I let myself in and you were mad at me for using my key? You guys were so busy panicking about Levi that you didn't even hear me open the door."

"Oh... shit." Lily's expression changes into a look I've never seen. And I love it.

"Oh, shit is right," I smirk.

"Let's talk about this in your truck." Another groan escapes her lips before she walks around my truck to the passenger side.

After I get in and the second I close my driver's side door, Lily presses the lock button and looks around the parking lot, as if someone cares enough to wonder what we're talking about in here. Her paranoid expression does wonders for what I am about to say to her.

"So what did you hear us talking about?" she asks.

"Exactly what I just told you. You're an accomplice to murder, sis."

"Well, sort of but not really. There's more to what you think you heard."

"Enlighten me."

Sighing, she sits up. "Okay, fine. But you can't repeat this to anyone."

After she fumbles an excuse about Jordan's business partner—the dead man named Levi, abusing his girlfriend and basically being a piece of shit person, I laugh.

"Why is this funny to you?" she snaps.

"So, you're telling me that your husband killed another man who was his own business partner because the dude was an abuser? I can understand the reason for not liking the guy but isn't that a little overboard? It's not like Levi abused *you*. What's it to Jordan that Levi beat up his own girlfriend? Why would that aggravate him enough to want to kill him?" I ask her in disbelief, but as the words escape my mouth, it becomes very obvious why Jordan wanted to kill the guy. "Oh wait! Was Levi's girlfriend also your husband's girlfriend? Was he cheating on you with her?"

The look on Lily's face tells me that she's thought about it except she shakes her head.

"No. No, he's not cheating."

"You sure about that?"

"Positive," she hesitates. "There's a bigger reason Jordan killed Levi. He was able to get some life insurance money when he died because they're business partners. Jordan is a beneficiary on Levi's insurance policy."

"Aha! Now things are starting to make a bit more sense," I smirk.

Money is a good motive to kill a person. It is also a good motive to blackmail a person too.

"So then, you're saying that Jordan used the abuser excuse to justify murdering his own partner because he knew he'd get money out of the guy's death?" My eyebrows raise.

She nods, silently.

"How much money?" I ask.

"Enough," she says.

"Okay, but what do you guys need money for? You look like you're living just fine to me."

Their two-story house in Coral Gables is fucking beautiful compared to my five hundred square foot apartment.

"Our financial situation is none of your business. So you can't tell anyone about this. Okay?" Lily nudges me, as if her gesture will force me to keep my mouth shut.

I huff a laugh. Without even knowing about Jordan's motive to get money out of Levi's death, I had my own similar motive in mind. Blackmail.

"Your secret is safe with me. Just give me three thousand dollars and I'll keep my mouth shut from calling the police on you two," I smile.

"I knew I shouldn't have told you about the money," Lily groans as she smacks her forehead.

"Oh, money was on my mind way before you just spilled your little secret."

"You're really going to extort me for money?" she huffs. "And why do you need three thousand dollars specifically?"

"My financial situation is none of your business, sis," I smirk.

"You're my brother! You'd really turn me into the police?"

I shrug.

"Whatever. I have no energy to argue with you right now. Don't talk to Jordan about this. You're going to have to wait until Friday for the money though. I have to make sure there's enough in my bank account."

"Your bank? Don't you share the same account with Jordan?"

"Yes, but I have my own savings account too."

"Oh, really?" I perk up at that. *More secrets.* "Does he know about it?"

"Don't worry about what he knows. I'll call you on Friday," she says while unlocking the door.

"Ah, well look at you two. You've got a secret savings account. You're killing people together. What a role model couple you two are."

"Would you shut up? I'm going home. You're not welcome to sleep over tonight either." She opens the passenger door, ready to make her escape.

Luckily, I don't really need to stay the night here in Miami. I only waited until Lily got out of work to talk to her because this was the perfect time to bombard her without the possibility of Jordan showing up. I actually really miss my bed. The five-hour drive home is not going to be fun, but it'll be worth it to sleep under my own blanket.

Before I can respond to Lily anyway, she gets out of my truck and is already quickly walking toward her own car in the parking lot.

I guess I will share the rest of my knowledge about Jordan's secret activity as a young adult when Lily gives me the money on Friday. Then I will demand even more money from her.

My sister will not get rid of me that easily. And now that I know about the money Jordan will receive soon, giving me three thousand dollars will be the least of their worries.

21

The party must go on

Richard's surprise birthday party is the last place I want to be right now. Still, me and Lily had an obligation to make an appearance tonight. I would have preferred to cancel this party since it is so soon after Levi died, but that was not my call to make because Gia planned the entire thing. She refused to cancel when I brought up the idea because she put down a non-refundable deposit to rent out the bar for three hours. In her words, the party must go on. Regardless of the fact that our friend died only two weeks ago.

Richard knows a lot of people. Double the amount of people than I do and triple more than Levi did. Unlike Levi, Richard isn't a piece of shit human being. That would probably be why Richard has so many friends. If I had to kill Richard, his death would be a lot more alarming to his several hundred friends and family. Thankfully, he isn't an asshole.

Speaking of murder, I received a call from Detective Shorty yesterday. He told me the investigation into Levi's death is now closed because the autopsy came back as a drowning. Just as I expected and as the results should be.

Now I am itching to put in a claim with the life insurance company for my money. But it would obviously be way too soon after the investigation closed, so I will have to wait at least another week to file. Even though the investigation is over, I can't let myself look suspicious.

I still have to talk Richard into filing with me also because it will look strange if I file alone. Before I killed Levi, I thought about how Richard would react to filing with me. I figured I would talk him into it without a problem when the time came. Monday, I'll bring it up to him in the office. I might even talk to Gia about it first, so in the event that Richard is hesitant, she can be on my side.

As for Levi's risen from the dead mother, neither Richard or I have heard from her. That seems a little odd that she has not tried to contact us because if she was so concerned about how her son died, wouldn't she want to talk to the people he was around right before he passed away? I am sort of expecting a sudden call from her or even worse, an uninvited visit at work. If that happens, I will just show her my remorse and get rid of her. Not *get rid of her*, get rid of her. Although getting rid of her for good would take away my frustrations. I meant, I'll just rush her off the phone or out of the office.

"I can't believe you still threw this party. There are so many people here. Doesn't it look a little inconsiderate to celebrate something so soon after your partner died?" Lily comes up to me with a margarita in her hand. "This does not look good on you and Richard."

"I'm not the one who threw this party. I helped plan it. This was all Gia, like I told you. Why don't you talk to her about it?" I nudge Lily's arm, knowing she doesn't want to talk to Gia.

"Rather not." Lily sips her drink.

Making the suggestion was strictly for my amusement. After a few more sips of her margarita, Lily will more than likely cave and go talk to her though because she gets too chatty, especially when she is drunk and curious. She'll likely annoy her too.

"Jordan Hoffman?" A perky unexpected voice alerts me from behind. "Oh, my God! We haven't seen each other in sooo long! How you been?"

Fuck. Being social doesn't bother me but tonight it does. I knew it was inevitable that I would have to socialize with people tonight, but that does not mean I want to, especially with a woman in front of my wife. I fight the urge to choke on my beer. I can't talk to another woman in front of my wife who was suddenly very suspicious of me cheating on her only a few weeks ago. Lily's self-esteem has dwindled and it shows.

"Good. Good. You?" I answer.

"Oh, I'm great!" She smiles.

"Hello," Lily clears her throat. "I'm Jordan's wife, Lily."

"Hi, I'm Sienna." She reaches out to shake Lily's hand.

As Lily returns the handshake, her glaring stare could burn a hole through Sienna's soul. Sienna is very pretty. Gorgeous, even more so than Gia is, who Lily was very jealous of. I can only imagine what is going through Lily's head right now. I think Gia and Sienna might even be around the same age which is also something my wife is probably not fond of. The insecurity is written all over Lily's face.

"Nice meeting you. I just came over to say hi, Jordan. Better get back to my friends." Sienna nods toward an area of the bar somewhere behind me, but I don't follow her gaze in the direction of whoever she is gesturing at.

My focus is on my insecure, impulsive wife who is staring daggers into that woman's back as Sienna walks away.

"Who was that?" The daggers are fixated on me now.

"Sienna. She's a friend of Richard and Gia's," I answer.

"Okay, but why does she know you?"

"Because she hired our company to help her move a while back."

"And she met you? I didn't know you meet all your clients."

"Well, no. I don't meet the clients. I only talk to them on the phone when I'm booking their moving appointments. I only met Sienna because she hired us right when we started the business. We didn't have enough movers at the time because they were all booked with other clients, so since she's friends with Richard, we just did it ourselves."

"SPEECH! SPEECH!" Suddenly the crowd shouts and we see Richard standing on top of the bar, double fisting two beers in his hands.

"Okay, let's put our happy faces on and get through these next few hours." I grab my wife's hand and navigate us through the crowd as she grips her emotional support margarita.

"Oh, I can't wait to celebrate the autopsy results tonight when we get home," she whispers.

"Let's save the celebration for after I file the insurance claim and the money goes through, honey. Just a few more weeks. Then we can really celebrate."

I am not one to be superstitious, but let's not celebrate too prematurely and jinx anything. I am almost out of the woods. I just need to make it there.

PART 3

22

Three and a half
weeks since the
murder

Plenty of time has passed since Levi died that it felt safe enough to file a claim with the life insurance company without raising any concerns. Richard and I finished filing this afternoon.

Even though the three of us all took policies out on each other when we first opened our moving company years ago, Richard forgot all about it. He didn't even remember that he is a beneficiary for each of us and had access to a payout as a business partner until I explained how the process worked to him and Gia.

I told them that receiving the money will help our business out in the long run by providing us funds for better moving trucks, equipment upgrades, and maybe even for their wedding. *It would be like Levi's wedding gift to you guys*, I told them. Richard seemed a bit skeptical at first until Gia said she thought it was a good idea, then he agreed.

So now that the last and most important part of my plan is completed, any suspicion revolving around the circumstance of Levi's death will not strictly fall on me.

That's if anyone is still apprehensive about how he died. The cause of death on Levi's autopsy came back as a drowning with alcohol intake as it should have, but I am not sure that I should trust whether the police believe that. Just because the investigation is officially closed now, does not mean the investigators have stopped their own speculations.

There is also Levi's absent ghost of a mother who I have to think about. Does she think I did something to her son because I was the only one who was alone on the beach with him when he died? I wonder if she thinks Richard was responsible for his death too, even though he wasn't even there. Or did she genuinely get worried about her son and wanted to make sure he died from an accident after all? Will I have to worry about her coming after me?

Let's hope not. I was only questioned by the two detectives once. They never spoke to Lily like they said they wanted. Thank God because if they did, I really would've been screwed. Maybe the interaction I had with the detectives just made me paranoid and I was never actually a suspect in the investigation to begin with. Everything they asked me about that night and had me reenact in my living room might have been all just protocol.

Regardless, what's done is done. There is no going back in time. The claim is filed. The investigation is over. I shouldn't have to worry about that part anymore.

Within sixty days, after the insurance company completes the claim, I will receive my portion of the payout. Then I will finally be able to pay off all the debt I incurred and put behind all of the mistakes that led me here. All the immense anxiety and stress I put on myself and had to take on during these past few months will finally be gone.

As long as nobody else gets in my way, my life will finally return to normal and nobody else should get hurt.

2 3

L i l y

I have never seen so much of my ignorant little brother's pain in the ass face until recently. Throughout the past few years, we only saw each other a couple of times before our mother passed away. After we reconciled our relationship, we only spoke on the phone once every week or two. The last time we saw each other in person before the car incident was at my mother's funeral. But now, Mike is suddenly interested in taking frequent road trips down here to Miami all the time. Lucky me.

If only our relationship stayed estranged. I wish I never trusted him with a key to my house. Mike is making me regret reconciling our relationship. Life would be a hell of a lot better and less stressful on my end if we hadn't.

Earlier this morning, he called to tell me he was on his way here instead of just showing up at my house or at my job unexpectedly this time around. I tried telling him he was not welcomed here, but my words did nothing because he still walked right through my front door a few minutes ago. He didn't even bother to knock. *Stupid key. And stupid me for trusting him.*

I should have changed the locks or taken the damn key away from him when he overheard mine and Jordan's conversation. I wouldn't be in this messy situation that is allowing Mike to blackmail me, if it weren't for me trusting him in the first place. This is just another example of how I never think things through. I did not think about whether trusting Mike was a good idea or not before just handing the key over. Now I have learned far too late that it was one of the worst decisions I have ever made.

While dressed in an all black sweatsuit with an obvious fake gold chain draped around his neck that he always wears, Mike sits down at my kitchen table. His hands clasped in front of him. "It's Friday. I'm here for my money."

"I tried telling you not to come here. I was just going to do a money transfer from my bank to yours. You didn't need to come here and act like you're a hitman demanding to be paid back for performing a kill," I say and I can't help but laugh. I am not sure if his outfit was purposely chosen for the occasion or not, but he is not intimidating me. Aggravating me, yes. Not intimidating.

"I don't want the money in my bank. You need to give it to me in all cash. Tax purposes," he says.

"Well, if you want cash then now you have to wait until Monday because the bank just closed. It's five-thirty already. I can't go get that much money out of an ATM at once either, so don't try asking me to go to one right now. There's a five-hundred-dollar limit at the ATM I normally go to. This is your fault for getting here so late in the day. Like I said, I tried telling you not to come here, but you didn't listen to me."

"Okay, that's fine. Waiting a few more days won't kill me," he smirks. "But Jordan might."

"Okay, you can leave now."

"No, no, not yet. Speaking of Jordan, I came here to talk to you about something else I know about him. It's something I'm not sure *you* even know about your husband."

"Like you care about what I know or don't know about Jordan," I sigh.

"Hey, no matter what you think, I do care about you, sis. That's why I want to talk to you about this."

"You're blackmailing me. You don't care about me or Jordan."

"That's half-true. I don't give a fuck about Jordan. And despite our distant relationship between me and you in the past, I do care about you. After all, you *are* my big sis," he grins.

"Right. So then, what else do you want to tell me about my husband now, huh?" Humouring Mike is my only option in this situation. Arguing will not get him to leave my house any faster, so I might as well play along with whatever game he is trying to play now.

He leans forward. "Did you know that Jordan murdered someone else before he killed Levi?"

Well, that was not what I was expecting Mike to say. If I weren't so irritated, I'd laugh. Instead, I let my eyes roll. He's fibbing. He's just trying to get a rise out of me. I am in no mood for his shit right now.

"Whatever you say, Mike."

"Aha! So, you don't know about what he did then? *Your* mother-in-law knows more about your husband than you do. I heard the two of them talking the last time I was here. Jordan said he got rid of his mother's boyfriend when he was younger. Not sure how old he was exactly when he killed the guy because he didn't specify his age, but he did say he was barely an adult. It's obvious he meant he killed somebody when he used the words *got rid of*, though. I mean, what else would he mean by that, right?"

"What are you talking about? You've never met Susan, his mom. You're making all this up."

"You're right. I haven't met her, but I heard her talking to Jordan the morning after I stayed the night. She was worried your husband became a killer after his first victim—whoever her boyfriend was. I was in the bathroom downstairs when I overheard them talking. She wanted to make sure he didn't kill Levi because you told her about Levi's drowning in the Keys. She got suspicious of her own son being the culprit of the poor guy's death."

I did tell Susan that Levi died during our camping trip because she wanted to know why Jordan didn't answer her call. I accidentally slipped and said he was talking to a detective which is why he didn't answer her. So when she asked me why a detective was on the phone with him, I had to tell her Levi died. That led to her asking me more questions and I did my best to answer them. I really didn't think telling her about Levi would be a big deal. Not that I told her how he actually died. I stuck to my story like I promised I would to Jordan. Susan was going to find out he died anyway. I never thought that would make her suspicious of Jordan because why on earth would she suspect her own son killed him?

Well, shit. This means, my brother isn't lying to me because Jordan's mom *did* come over the morning after Mike spent the night. I heard Susan shout to me when I was getting ready for work right before I came downstairs. Mike was already gone by then.

But even though that's all true, he has to be bluffing about what he presumably heard during Jordan and Susan's conversation. Since Mike knows Jordan killed Levi, he probably just came up with an elaborate lie because he can. He's lying because he is conniving and he hates my husband. That's all.

"You're lying," I challenge, gritting the back molars of my teeth.

"You know, you guys aren't really smart when it comes to this whole murder thing and for a married couple, you don't communicate well either. Why didn't you tell Jordan I stayed the night? He had no idea I was in the bathroom, eavesdropping on his conversation until he walked in on me after his mother left."

"I thought I did tell him."

Didn't I?

"No... yes. I did tell him," I shake my head and stand up. "He probably forgot what I said. Or maybe he thought you already left the house since he didn't see you on the couch when he was downstairs."

"You two are something else," Mike huffs, shaking his head. "So now, about that money you owe me. Since I know that added fact about your killer husband, an extra two thousand will be sufficient enough to keep my mouth shut about his first victim and Levi."

"Have you lost your mind?" I nearly shout, my mouth hanging slightly open.

"Okay, I'll settle with an extra thousand instead. Call it even," Mike smirks.

There is no sense in arguing with Mike. He isn't going to budge and I have no other option. There's no way I am going to allow him to go to the police and turn in Jordan. Or me for being an accomplice to Levi's murder. Thankfully, I have my secret savings account to pay him off so he can keep his mouth shut. Because how else would I explain when four thousand dollars goes missing out of the bank to Jordan?

"Fine. Four thousand dollars and that's it. This conversation is over. I'll take the money out of the bank on Monday and give it to you then. You know, you not only wasted my time and yours, but you wasted gas coming here too. Now you're going to have to drive back and forth again since you won't allow me to transfer the money to your bank. Your logic makes no sense."

"Road trips don't really bother me anyway. Besides, I'll be raking in four thousand dollars soon. Spending a little gas money won't break my bank come Monday," Mike winks. "But listen, you need to be careful around Jordan. Your husband's an actual murderer. Doesn't matter what reason he is using to justify killing people. Find out who his first victim was. His mom said it happened over twenty years ago."

"Jordan's not a murderer. Well, actually—yes, he kind of is, but he only killed Levi. It's not like he's a killer-killer."

"Are you hearing yourself right now?" Mike stands up. "Other than what I just told you, what makes you think your husband has never killed anyone else before he murdered Levi? A normal person does not decide to kill people just for the hell of it. Not for a payout from insurance and not because the dude was just a shitty guy. There's got to be more to it than that. Unless like I said before, Jordan was fucking around with Levi's girlfriend and he got all protective when he found out Levi beat her. See, that would seem like a better excuse for why he offed the guy."

No. No. No. Mike is wrong. Jordan has not killed anyone else. That's unbelievable... But cheating? Cheating was my initial thought. That was my initial intuition until he proved that Gia wasn't his mistress...

Now that I think about it, Mike might be making a good point. What if my husband killed Levi because Sharon was his mistress after all? I've never met the woman. The first time I heard about her was when Jordan confessed his murder plan to me. And that was only after I told him about my plan to shoot Gia. He only told me he planned to kill Levi because of what I was going to do to Gia...

No. No. No! What the hell am I thinking? Mike is just getting in my head. My husband is not cheating on me. Jordan said he isn't and never has. He never will. He told me that on the beach after I accused him of being unfaithful to me with Gia. I need to trust him.

"Since I'm in town again, you might as well let me stay the night," Mike walks over to my linen closet next to the downstairs bathroom to pull out a bed sheet. He's already getting himself settled in for the night.

"No! Jordan will throw a fit if you stay here. Find a hotel tonight or drive back home." I try to grab the sheet out of his hands, but he yanks it away.

"What's he gonna do? Kill me?" Mike grins. "Listen I can just go to the police—"

"—Okay, okay, fine. You can stay the night. Just be quiet and try to leave before he wakes up so you two won't cross paths in the morning."

"I'll do my best to avoid the killer." Mike walks into the living room, then throws the bed sheet on the couch. "I'm just getting my bed ready for when I come back, sis. I think I'll go sight-see around South Beach for the night. Don't worry about leaving the door unlocked for me," he laughs as he waves my house key in the air. He passes my crooked wedding picture on the wall, looks at it while shaking his head, then leaves through the front door.

As the door closes, I wait for our wedding photo to fall on the ground per usual, but surprisingly, the heavy frame remains in place. Looks like Jordan finally replaced the nail in the wall. It only took him about a month to listen to me.

I walk into the kitchen to grab a bottle of wine from the fridge. I did not plan on drinking tonight but after my conversation with Mike, I changed my mind.

My mind is all over the place now. *Cheating...* Was my husband cheating on me with Sharon? Did he actually kill another person when he was younger? Or was Mike just trying to extort me for more money by coming up with such an elaborate lie?

Then again, if my brother wanted more than the three-thousand-dollars he originally demanded from me, then he didn't need to lie about anything after all. He could have just threatened to turn in Jordan and myself to the police instead. An exaggerated lie isn't needed to get me to give into giving him more of my money...

Oh my God.

Got rid of...

Why didn't I pick up on that phrase right away?

Those words are too specific to the words Jordan used when he explained his murder plan on the beach to me. He told me he planned to *get rid of Levi.*

Mike isn't lying about Jordan after all.

2 4

Why would Jordan kill Susan's boyfriend when he was younger? And why the hell didn't Jordan ever tell me about him? It would not be very wise of me to straight up ask Susan about any of her exes, but what I can do, is look through their family photo albums. Maybe I will find a picture of whoever the guy is. I mean, whoever he *was*.

His mom gave us all of her family photo albums years ago when she moved from her old house to an apartment down the street from us. She didn't have enough space in her new place so we stored them in our garage for her. If I want to find out who the guy is, I can only think to look for the boyfriend Mike heard about in a picture. I need to start searching through the album that dates back to when Jordan was around eighteen or so, given the information Mike told me he eavesdropped on.

Twenty years ago, Jordan would have been twenty-years old because he is forty now. He told me he moved out of Susan's house when he was nineteen.

Jordan was sixteen years old when his parents got divorced. He never told me about any of Susan's boyfriends following the divorce though. He did say his father was abusive and that's why his parents ended up separating. But Jordan never really elaborated on how abusive his father was (whether it was physical or mental, not that it matters) or whatever really happened between his parents. I never asked about the details regarding his parents' relationship either. Mainly because Jordan never volunteered any information about them.

Come to think of it, Jordan's reason for wanting to kill Levi makes even more sense now. How did I not put two and two together? Jordan's family history with his father completely slipped my mind. That further sends me to believe he isn't cheating on me as Mike suggested. Jordan really was angry at Levi for the way he treated Sharon and his anger led him to murder. Just as Jordan told me. He wasn't protecting Sharon because he was having an affair with her. Mike is wrong about that.

I'm going to kill him for messing with my head about my marriage. Other than that, Mike might be right about everything else he told me though and right now, I'm going to confirm whether all of it is true or not.

In the garage, I find a small green storage bin that contains two photo albums. The top one is Jordan's baby album. I've looked through this one in the past. But I haven't looked through the second album which dates back to Jordan's teenage years.

Flipping through the pages, I find less appearances from his father in the photos as

Jordan gets older, and more appearances of a few different men. Three different guys in total. This happens around the age of sixteen, right after his parent's got divorced. I assume these men must be Susan's ex-boyfriends.

Out of the three men, one of them who is a couple inches taller, pale and very skinny with dark scraggly hair takes up more space in this album than the other two guys pictured. There is a picture of Jordan when he looks to be around eighteen or nineteen with Susan and the skinny guy. They're standing somewhere in North Beach, Miami. On the back of the picture, Susan wrote the words, "me" meaning her, Jordan, and Jerry. On the next page, I spot a photo of Susan and Jerry on a couch, alone. Then another photo shows Jerry by himself, grilling in a backyard.

A Google lens search on one of these photos might help me find more information on this Jerry guy.

Utilizing the search option, I snap a picture with my phone of the photograph showing Jerry grilling and await the results. The photo is not one-hundred percent clear, but it's clear enough to distinguish his facial features.

A long page of results shows up under the Google lens search. I easily spot an image from a Facebook profile that appears in the list of results. It's an old photo of a man who looks identical to Jerry. By the quality of the image, it is obvious that the photo was either scanned to be posted online or taken with a phone camera as I just did. The rest of the images in the result list are clearer and concise, easily telling me they were all photographed over the past decade as opposed to two decades ago.

On the Facebook post with Jerry's picture which is dated back to three months ago, the caption reads: *In memory of my brother, Jerry. I miss you, big brother. Twenty-two years without you.*

Twenty-two years ago, Jordan would have been eighteen years old...

Eighteen years old sounds most appropriate to the phrase *barely an adult.*

Before jumping to conclusions though, I should find out how Jerry died. Just because he passed away doesn't mean my husband was responsible for—

Oh, or maybe it does.

A further google search provides me access to Jerry's public death record.

His cause of death: *an accidental fall causing injury to his head while under the influence of alcohol intoxication.*

An accidental death...

Alcohol intoxication...

That sounds too similar to how Jordan staged *"Levi's accident"* on the beach.

This isn't a coincidence after all. Mike was right. My husband really did kill two people...

But is Mike right about him cheating on me too?

2 5

A woman's intuition never lies

Although I am ninety-nine percent certain Jordan killed Jerry, I am not as infuriated at him for being a murderer as I was when I thought he was cheating on me with Gia. I am actually intrigued... and equally confused. Also, I am a little bit worried. Not worried that he could potentially harm me. I'm mostly concerned about the circumstances of his first victim, Jerry. What exactly happened that led Jordan to kill his mother's boyfriend back then? He never told me about that which is aggravating that he could keep such a secret. Why wouldn't he tell me?

I have never even heard stories about his mother dating after his parents divorced. I assumed she did, but I hadn't the slightest clue or interest in how her love life went. Just because the topic of conversation never came up, that doesn't mean Jordan had the right to keep his secret from me though.

Wait a second... Does this mean Jordan is a serial killer because he killed two people?

According to a quick Google search, yes, he is. The definition of a serial killer is to kill more than one person.

Well shit. I married an actual serial killer. My husband killed Levi for a good reason though so technically, he is a good serial killer. A Dexter kind of killer, one who seeks revenge on those who deserve it, if there is such a thing.

Okay, I can live with that.

What I would have preferred to live without is knowing about Jerry's death, but Mike had to meddle. He just had to get in mine and my husband's business. I love my little brother. I also can't stand him at the same time. If I tell Jordan that Mike knows about Jerry, he'll lose his mind. He might even kill Mike for simply eavesdropping on his conversation...

Or worse, Jordan might get so angry at me and Mike together for both knowing about what he's done in the past, then Jordan might want to kill me too...

No. No. No! What the hell am I thinking? Jordan is my husband! He would never harm me! Maybe he would murder Mike to keep his secret, but me? No way! Jordan trusted me with Levi's murder, so why would it matter if he found out I know about Jerry?

Then again, Jordan never told me about Jerry and probably never plans to say anything either. Sixteen years of being together have gone by after all. If he ever had plans to tell me about Jerry, the subject would have come up by now. So, no. Of course he never intended to tell me about his first victim and most likely never will. That's probably because he thinks he can't trust me...

And as I think about it, he was never going to tell me about his plan to murder Levi. He only confessed after he realized how serious I was about shooting Gia. Jordan's whole plan was to use me as an alibi—a witness, along with the others that night. He was going to keep all of us in the dark, especially his own wife.

That angers me even more.

Now I have no idea what to believe. Between my dirtbag brother's insinuation of my husband being unfaithful and my mother-in-law's deceased boyfriend, a myriad of questions are being brought to my attention. Questions that have never come across my mind until now. And I hate that. Because now I need answers.

Can I really trust my husband? Can I trust everything he has ever told me, especially what he said about Levi?

He said he wanted to kill Levi because he abused Sharon which would give him reason to kill him. The payout from the life insurance money ended up being an added bonus... to pay off his debt—debt that I am still unsure of what is even for.

Unless... unless my husband was lying about part of that. Was the fifty-thousand-dollar payout Jordan's entire reason to kill him and Levi wasn't an abuser after all?

Maybe he just said that to make me feel better, to justify his reason for killing him.

Or worse—Is Mike's allegation that Jordan was cheating on me with Sharon, along with my inner woman's intuition, correct? Was my husband protecting his mistress? Besides battling Jordan's childhood trauma of seeing his mother get abused by his father, that *would* give Jordan more of a plausible reason to kill Levi after all.

My intuition had me believing that Jordan had an affair with Gia, but maybe Gia wasn't the other woman he was cheating with. Maybe Sharon *is* the other woman...

Fuck Mike for getting inside my head!

Thud. And fuck our wedding picture that keeps falling off the wall. I thought Jordan replaced the loose nail with a new one. Clearly, I was wrong. It's as if our fallen wedding photo is a symbolic sign—a sign my marriage is falling apart right in front of my eyes.

Screw it. I'll just remove the nail and hammer a new one in the wall myself. That way I will never have to ask Jordan to do it again. I'm tired of asking him to do things around the house and they never get done. Now is a good time as any to hammer away my stress right now anyway!

Sorry nail! You're about to feel the wrath of my fury tonight.

Time to find the hammer which should be in Jordan's nightstand in our bedroom.

Upstairs, I rummage through the drawer of the nightstand to find my stress reliever. His drawer is filled with a messy pile of loose papers and God knows what else is in here. Hopefully, the damn hammer. I have seen Jordan toss it in here on multiple occasions, so it must still be in here now.

No idea why he keeps the hammer in his drawer and not in the garage with the rest of his tools, but he does.

In his drawer, the mess of papers contain scribblings with a variety of numbers and calculations that I assume are for our finances. Jordan normally jots down our bills in a notebook before bed every Friday night. Another thing he does that makes no sense to me; he goes over our bills right before he falls asleep. That seems a little absurd because what psycho would want to stress themselves out about finances right before going to bed?

But then again, I clearly have no idea why my husband does a lot of things. And after all, he is a psycho.

Aha! There it is! The small black hammer sticks out underneath a really old coffee-stained notebook; the spiral spine is almost broken all the way off the pad.

Okay, finally it's hammer time! Right after I go look for the box of nails on a shelf in the garage. The box must be in the garage because Jordan has not touched them in a long time. Hence, my countless requests to replace the nail in the wall.

Oh, wait a second...

What. The. Fuck!

Just as I am closing his drawer, some of the loose papers shift inside and an iPhone box is revealed in the corner, right near another notebook.

This has to be an empty box because Jordan does not own an iPhone...

Oh, never mind. Apparently, he does.

Why the hell does he have this thing? And why is it turned off?

Well, time to turn it on and find out.

My inner woman's intuition is screaming at me right now. What the hell am I about to find on here?

The password that he uses to unlock his regular phone, which is an out-of-date android that he refuses to upgrade (my husband, the cheap ass strikes again) unlocks this one.

I know his password because there is nothing we keep hidden from each other.

Or so I thought we didn't hide anything from each other...

If he wanted to hide this phone from me, then why would he use his regular password to unlock it? Is he really that ignorant? Or maybe it is because he trusts me so much that he knows I would never snoop through his drawer. Or he takes me as an idiot because he knows I trust him so much (well, that was true until his conversation with Gia made me jump to conclusions). He probably wouldn't think twice about me snooping through his things. He also knows I never open this drawer because there is never a need for me to. This is his junk drawer.

Same as my side, there is no reason for him to go through my stuff.

Well jokes on him because I wasn't even snooping through his drawer on purpose. This is his fault for procrastinating in re-hanging our picture and keeping the hammer here. If he didn't want me to see this phone, he should have simply listened to my several requests to fix the damn nail in the wall! If the hammer was kept in the garage where it should be, his secret phone would not be unlocked in my hand right now. This is all his fault.

First, I check through his text messages, hoping this phone was a gift from Richard or someone and he hasn't actually used it yet.

Oh, but no... My hopes quickly get shut down the second the screen unlocks and I open his messages. Only one text message thread appears. The contact he's been texting with is from an 'S'. No picture. Just an 'S'.

S? S for Sharon?

I drop myself on the edge of the bed, my heart hammering in my chest. My legs all of a sudden are too weak to keep myself upright. My eyes are glued to the phone screen. Lasered in on the font.

My intuition, my intuition was right all along. Yet still, my eyes can't comprehend the words they're reading in my hand.

What...the...hell am I looking at?!

Without scrolling up on their conversation, the most recent messages are visible on the screen. The last text was sent a month and a half ago.

From Jordan: **Meet me at my office tomorrow.**

Reply from S: **What for?**

From Jordan: **I have a surprise for you. It'll be my last one. Then we can never speak or see each other again. I've given you enough. It's over after this. I never want to see you again. I mean it.**

Reply from S: **We'll see about that.**

Furiously, I scroll all the way up until the conversation doesn't allow me to scroll anymore. To the very first text message dated back to eight months ago.

From S: **Can't wait to see you again.**

From Jordan: **I miss you.**

From S: **Stopping in later for lunch.**

From S: **Be there in ten.**

From Jordan: **Can't wait. Heart emojis.**

From S: **Kiss emojis.**

From Jordan: **Last night was fun. Can't wait to do it again. *Wink emoji.* *Heart eyes emoji. * *Eggplant emoji***

The eggplant emoji? Really?!

No. No. No. No! How disgraceful to find out my forty-year-old husband is having an affair and even worse, he is using a damn eggplant emoji through sexting! How despicable!

I keep scrolling up to read all these appalling messages—more despicable emoji's and outrageous, horrifying sexting between them until I see a picture sent to Jordan from the mysterious 'S'.

What. The. Fuck.

Not just one, but *four* photos of a naked bitch who had the nerve to introduce herself to me were sent to Jordan. Multiple times. In multiple positions.

As the saying goes—a woman's intuition is always right and mine was right all along. My pathetic murderous husband is having an affair after all.

2 6

My desire to kill somebody is back in motion. This time, my target is Jordan.

How dare he have the audacity to lie to my face like that when I accused him of cheating on me with Gia? Sure, I had accused him of cheating with the wrong bitch but still! He had the nerve to say the words *'never have'*, *'never will'* to me! That's overkill! Literally a gun to my face. All he had to do was pull the trigger.

Actually, he did pull the trigger already. He pulled it when he allowed me to shake hands with that young twenty looking something bitch who introduced herself as Sienna at Richard's party. My blood boils at the thought of me touching another woman who has intimately touched him! I could kill the home wrecking whore too.

But right now, my focus is solely on getting rid of Jordan, as he would call it. I can figure out how to get rid of Sienna or Sharon—whatever the hell her real name is, afterward. At this point, I am not even sure if Sharon is a real person or if she is actually the woman in the photos on this iPhone—the same person who introduced herself as Sienna at Richard's party.

My brother might have been right all along. Maybe Jordan really did kill Levi because he abused his mistress. Maybe Jordan used the name *Sharon* instead of Sienna to hide her true identity. I bet Jordan probably came up with the name *Sharon* because he thought I would never actually meet Sienna. I bet he didn't think she would come to Richard's party... or did he?

After all, Jordan didn't look the teeniest bit shocked when Sienna walked right up and said hello to him. Let's not forget she ignored me at first until I announced my presence. Then again, Jordan is clearly a professional liar so I don't know what to think. He is experienced enough to keep me blindsided by his lies for the entirety of our relationship. Blindsided not only by his affair, but by his murderous past too.

A flood of questions are running through my mind. Although one thing I am sure of is that Jordan is definitely having an affair with the naked woman in the photos. Regardless of whatever the hell her real name is. And Jordan is going to pay for being unfaithful to me. Unlike when I initially thought Gia was his mistress, this Sienna/Sharon bitch is not the first target on my hit list this time around.

When I thought Jordan was cheating with Gia, I was ready to kill her because I figured we would be able to somehow work through his infidelity. Various scenarios of killing him appeared in my mind, but I could never bring myself to act on those fantasies. My rage only made me imagine scenarios where I could kill my husband. That was all.

Now I no longer think that way! My rage will definitely allow me to kill Jordan this time! Screw working through his infidelity. We will not be able to work through all the lies and secrets he's kept from me during our sixteen years of being together. Not especially after he watched me speak to his mistress like it was no big deal and worst of all, he looked me in the face and said he never cheated on me and never will.

He did not only cheat once. He was having a full-blown affair for at least eight months according to those text messages. The affair could have even been going on for longer than that, who knows!

How. Dare. He!? What else has he withheld from me?

Now I am not even sure if the personal expense he had to pay for his business—supposedly to cover some vague equipment and problem with a client was ever real to begin with. Was that a lie to cover up his other lies? Does ten thousand dollars in debt even exist?

I intend to figure all that out right the fuck now. His credit report and score should answer all of my questions.

Thankfully, I know his social security number, so logging into a credit app that will give me all the access to what is on his credit report appears easily on my phone.

The report tells me his score is average. Not high. Not too low either. So then, how many loans does he owe? According to what he told me, he took out a couple different business loans when he opened the moving company. They're all supposed to be paid off within the next two years.

And there they are. Those loans actually exist. Okay, so he didn't lie about that. But there is also a credit card on here... A credit card that was supposed to be paid off by now. It shows he—actually *we*, owe two-thousand and three hundred dollars on it. We used this card for groceries and miscellaneous items before. Jordan said we paid it off last year and we should only use it for emergencies.

But no, this is just another thing he lied about! He's been using it this whole time! None of these charges look like they were for emergencies.

There are a list of recent charges dating back to about eight months ago on this card. Charges at several restaurants and bars, but mostly at the bar where Richard's party was held. All of these charges are around thirty to seventy dollars each. *What the fuck! So much for being a cheapass!*

He had to have used this card for whenever he took his mistress out on dates because I sure as hell have never stepped foot in that bar until Richard's party was thrown. We haven't gone out to any bars or a restaurant together in probably about a year now either, so none of these charges were spent on me!

I'm livid. What the fuck else is he hiding?

Since we both share this credit card, I should check my own credit score. With my name attached to his, my score must have gone down because of all those ridiculous extra charges. Not that my credit score really matters at this point. I should still check on it though.

Between the cheating, killing, and now the debt, I can't become any more infuriated.

Oh wait... I take that back because yes, the fuck I can! Forget the credit card!

Right after I log into the app with my own credentials and social security number, an auto loan for ten thousand dollars hits me in the face. I'm blindsided. I never applied for an auto loan, let alone one for ten thousand dollars. My twenty-year-old car has been paid off for years and it's not even worth half as much as that!

Ten thousand dollars.

Now everything is starting to make sense. All of Jordan's lies are connecting. He doesn't owe ten thousand dollars for any equipment pertaining to his business, as he told me in the Keys. He owes the money for a car he bought. He must have taken the loan out in my name because his score is so low that the loan company wouldn't approve him. And he knows my social security number so it wasn't hard to apply for one without my knowledge. I never check my credit score either and he knows that.

Whatever vehicle he bought had to have been for his mistress because Jordan hasn't been driving around in a new car and I'm still driving my shitty Corolla. The loan was taken out last month. I know the new car was definitely not bought for me and I doubt he is hiding it somewhere to give me as a present either. My cheap ass husband complains about a twelve-dollar margarita. He would never buy me anything, let alone a ten-thousand-dollar car.

Oh, but it seems more likely he gladly spent that money in my name for his side piece, that young home wrecking whore!

A quick call to the loan company tells me what I did not want to hear. Although, their response was inevitable. As it stated on my credit report, he applied for the loan last month to pay for a Lexus that is ten years old.

How dare he buy a car—one that is in way better shape than mine is, for another fucking woman? And even worse, the car loan is under my damn name! It's like I bought the damn thing for her!

Actually, no. *We* bought it for her. Because any debt I incur, Jordan does too. That is how marriages work. What's mine is yours. Did my idiot husband not realize my debt is his debt too? Or is that something he realized far too late and that's when he truly decided killing Levi will end all of his problems? I saw the check from the life insurance company, so that is one thing

Jordan did not lie about. He really was a beneficiary.

Although nothing matters at this point, I need to find out if Sienna and Sharon are the same person before I kill my husband. Then I will decide if killing the home wrecking whore will be worth my energy afterward.

2 7

My lack of foresight has to change

While getting myself ready to head to the restaurant and dreading the upcoming workday, I come downstairs to find Jordan sitting in the kitchen at the dining table. My purse is right in front of him, unzipped. Several wads of cash rolled up by a rubber band reveals itself—four thousand dollars that is meant for Mike when he meets me at work today.

"Where did all this money come from?" Jordan asks as he sips his coffee.

I blame Mike for this. If only my scheming brother allowed me to send the money that he is extorting out of me directly to his bank account, I would not be in this predicament with Jordan.

Then again, this *is* also my fault for leaving four thousand dollars out in my purse on the table like this. But in my defense, I never thought Jordan would look in my purse because he never has. Did I leave it unzipped or did he unzip it himself? If he did unzip my purse, then why the hell was he snooping in my bag? He's never done that. At least, not that I know of.

"Oh, I took some money out from my bank. I've always had a savings account. I—"

"—But why did you take so much money out?" He cuts me off, either forgoing the fact that I just mentioned a savings account that was unknown to him or simply because he doesn't care about the account at all. Maybe he *did* know about my savings account all along and again, he just doesn't care. He clearly does not care about me anymore nor does he care about our marriage.

Well, what do I say now? I was not prepared for him to see the money. I should have never left my purse alone down here while I was getting ready for work. This is just another consequence I'm faced with for not thinking things through. I should have hidden the money in a better inconspicuous spot, like in another zipper inside my purse, or in an envelope. Or better yet, I shouldn't have even kept any of it in my purse at all.

My lack of foresight has to change. Especially when I kill my cheating bastard of a husband. My whole plan has to be calculated and executed accordingly. No room for mistakes or setbacks. My rage will not overcome my emotions. This time, my rage will drive me to think rationally when I murder my soon to be ex-husband.

"Mike needed to borrow money from me," I finally say. The half-truth could work. Technically, that isn't a lie. Mike does need the money; whatever he may need it for. He did not ask to borrow the money, more so demanded it in a threatening way, but Jordan doesn't need to know that.

"The fuck does he need four thousand dollars for?" Jordan huffs.

So he didn't just notice the lump sum of money, he counted all of it too. *Shit.*

"Uh, he needs... he needs rent money. He's behind this month."

"Wasn't he just here for a job that took a whole weekend? Didn't they pay him? And what apartment charges four thousand dollars a month for rent in Jacksonville? It's not like he lives in a luxury apartment building down here." Jordan's eyebrows furrow.

Okay, he makes a good point. We went to Mike's apartment after my mother's funeral since it was held only ten minutes away from him. His place definitely did not look like it costs four thousand dollars to rent out a month. Maybe two thousand at best.

"Well, yes, he did have a job somewhere in Homestead when he stayed here with us, but I don't know how much that job paid him. I'm not even sure if they paid him for his work yet. He just told me he needed rent or else his landlord would evict him. Come to think of it, you're actually right. Mike must be behind two months instead of only one because he was threatened with an eviction notice. He showed it to me."

"But why did you—"

"—Yeah, you know what? That does make more sense why he asked me for so much money," I say in an attempt to stop

Jordan from asking more questions. "I didn't really question him when he asked. I just said I'd lend him the money. I know he's annoying but I don't want him to be homeless. Imagine if he got evicted? Then he'd just want to stay with us and I know you don't want that to happen."

As I've said, thinking things through does not always come easily to me. Lying on the spot is a bit easier though. As long as I can keep my composure.

"I didn't know you have a savings account." Jordan looks down at the money. "How much do you have saved up?"

And I never knew you had a bitch on the side, a murder hobby, and was such a deceitful liar. I can't even tell if what he just said is a lie, he's that good. He could have known about my savings account all along and never said a word about it.

"Oh, the account is just for emergencies. A hundred bucks gets deposited from my paycheck into the bank every week. Actually, the four thousand was most of the money I had saved up. There's only about two hundred dollars left in the bank now."

That part is true. Mike basically cleaned my bank account out. If I had never spent money on my New York getaway, there would be more in my account after taking out the money for Mike. But again, Jordan does not know that.

Hmm, or does he?

Who the fuck knows anymore.

"Oh okay," is all Jordan responds. "He better pay you back soon though." He stands up from the table. "Why didn't you just transfer the money to his account? This is a lot of cash. It's not safe for you to walk around with it."

"Because he didn't want me to transfer it," I shrug. "I don't know why. I didn't ask questions. I'm working on trying to trust him more. He'll pay me back though. Don't worry. I'll see you later. I'm running late for work."

I grab my purse off the table and leave the kitchen. At the front door, I grab my keys from the hook off the wall, right next to the loose nail where our fallen wedding picture is supposed to be hanging. I never hammered my frustrations away and put the photo back up after I found Jordan's secret iPhone. The photo can stay on the ground from now on, for all I care. Hell, I might even throw it in the trash soon. It's not like Jordan will care or notice.

"Love you. Have a good day at work," Jordan says from behind me and I realize that he just walked me to the front door.

Well, this is strange. He has not done this in a long time. He used to walk me to the door every time I left for work in the morning and kiss me goodbye. He usually leaves a few minutes after me. I am just now realizing he stopped doing that months ago. It might have been in even almost a whole year ago... until right now. He is suddenly acting like he cares about me again. As if he still loves me.

But I know better than to fall for his act. For the first time in our fifteen years of marriage, I feel repulsed as we kiss goodbye. Killing him is going to be the best day of my life.

2 8

Time to plan for the perfect retaliation

On my way to work, my thoughts drift off to suffocating my husband in his sleep. Then to poisoning him at dinner. I imagine what it would feel like to shoot him over and over and over again right in the chest with his own gun. I picture a pool of blood surrounding his stomach as he lies face down on my beige living room carpet.

As desperately as I would love for each one of those imaginative scenarios to happen though, they unfortunately can't become a reality. His death cannot be proven it was done in such an obvious homicidal way.

Killing Jordan has to be thoroughly thought out. Just like he tried to do when he planned to kill Levi. Jordan made mistakes though. The first mistake was failing to realize that a missing person is not a dead person. If it weren't for me telling him that he can't file a claim with the life insurance company when a person is labeled missing and not dead, Jordan would not have received a payout, had he let Levi drift off in the ocean as he originally wanted to.

Jordan's second mistake was ignorantly believing Levi's story about his parents being dead. Jordan's ignorance carelessly caused an investigation, which led him to undergo police questioning because one of his parents is actually alive. What an idiot! For someone who committed murder a second time, you'd think he would have covered his tracks and been better at it than that.

Even though there were a few bumps in Jordan's plan and he almost failed, he succeeded by the skin of his teeth. That will not happen to me. I will not go through the tribulations that Jordan went through. There will not be any hiccups in my murder plan. Everything will go smoothly when I kill him because I am going to take my time. I will not impulsively rush into anything. Unlike my ignorant husband, I will cover all my tracks and prepare to kill him properly.

Ironically, Jordan's motive to receive his life insurance payout from Levi's death has unintentionally become my plan now. Well, sort of. The money is not driving me to kill him, of course, but it is an added bonus. You can call it my reward. My reward for being mistook as a blind idiot throughout our marriage.

Jordan and I took out spousal life insurance policies on each other. So after he dies, no matter what the circumstances are (as long as it's proven I didn't kill him) it will be inevitable for me to receive a payout. I haven't looked into the details of our policies since we set them up early on in our marriage, but I think the amount of money we would each receive in the event one of us dies is around a hundred and fifty thousand dollars—enough to secure a peaceful future for myself without him for a long time.

Even though there will not be an investigation after his murder, I will not risk looking up the details of the insurance policy. My sudden online research history could make me look like a suspect in his death and I will not allow that to happen. No need to give the authorities any reason to look at me. Aside from my own common sense, plenty of movies have taught me not to look anything up on the internet before committing a crime.

See, I'm starting to think things through before acting on my decisions! Speaking of thinking before acting, I have decided Jordan's mistress does not deserve my energy and time. Her life will be spared from my wrath of fury.

The home wrecking whore can mourn my husband's death and endure any karma the world may stow upon her in the future by her lonesome. Jordan is the cheating lying bastard who deserves to die in this situation. Although his side piece is no better, and had the nerve to introduce herself to me when she obviously knew who I was, the bitch can endure the consequences of her choices differently. She will grieve her secret lover in private. She will not be granted the wish to bestow her grief upon anyone about him or in public because she was the side bitch—the secret. Suffering in silence all alone in private will be a torture in itself.

Now as for getting rid of Jordan (what a poetically classy way he would call it) a few, somewhat realistic and exciting options come to mind. My retaliation tactic needs to be just right. Jordan's death has to be conclusive. He has to die in a way that will not prompt any unnecessary questions and speculations.

Stabbing him in his back or anywhere in the front of his body would be satisfying, except that would look like a straight up obvious homicide to the police. That would also take a lot of strength that I do not have. And there would be too much cleanup.

I could go with the self-defense excuse but that won't work either because the police would investigate me afterward. Or at least, they would question me. I would have to come up with a story that would just take up too much creativity, rehearsal, and memorization. There has never been any history of domestic abuse in our relationship. No domestic dispute police reports have been filed as evidence that would support my words. Nobody in mine or Jordan's life would back me up either. As much as playing the role of the beaten wife might sound most logical, self-defense would not work in my favor without any support.

Poisoning Jordan sounds fun. It would likely be a better option except that is not as easy as it sounds because I have no idea what to poison him with. And again, I know better than to look anything up on the internet and potentially implicate myself as a suspect. So no, no poisoning. Overdosing would be good if we had prescription pills in this house, especially if he had some in his name. But neither of us does. Sadly, we are perfectly healthy.

What I would do to have a bad back right now. Or a mental health issue. If only I had a condition that would provide me a cabinet full of prescription pills. I would lace his drink with half a bottle. Make it look like a suicide because he was so distraught after Levi's death. Or I'd be able to combine the pills with his tequila. Make it look like he took too many on accident...

An accident.

Aha! How poetic! I was so engrossed in thinking about the perfect technique when the answer was in front of my face all along!

I'll take a page out of Jordan's book. If only I could consult the master in staging accidental deaths, but no, no. I got this myself. I'm already on a role. This is my time to shine!

Jordan's death will look like a drunken accidental fall. Sort of like how he claimed Jerry died. I'll make it look like Jordan drank himself, literally to death. It will look like he mourned Levi so hard and became so overwhelmed by survivor's guilt because he couldn't rescue him from drowning on the beach in time. An alcoholic accident seems fitting.

Jerry's death was labeled as an intoxicated accident from falling and Levi's death was ruled out as a drowning due to intoxication. In both circumstances, the police believed the now deceased were so drunk that they basically killed themselves.

I can make the police think the same thing happened to Jordan. And nobody should question the circumstances of his death as long as he doesn't die in a similar way that Levi died. Both of their deaths cannot somehow fall on me as long as I am careful. As for Jerry's death, that happened over two decades ago. Jordan was clearly never under the police radar for that situation, so when I make Jordan look like he died from a similar accident, there shouldn't be any links to each other. No questions. No theories. I just have to do this right.

The only person who might question a thing or two will be Susan, but to her knowledge, I am unaware of Jordan's first victim, Jerry. In Susan's eyes, her son's death will simply be a coincidence. An unfortunate coincidence. As far as I know, Susan and Jordan are both under the assumption that I have no idea who Jerry even was. And as long as I keep my mouth shut, they will keep thinking that way.

The setting will be perfect. Since Jordan just received the insurance payout, I'll talk him into going out for a celebratory date night. We'll take an Uber to go out to eat and have a few drinks, which I will have to remind him that we can splurge because his natural response will be to say, "No. We should save some money." *Cheap ass.* Then we'll come home to share a bottle of wine in the living room.

I will pretend to get drunk like how he pretended to drink with Levi on the beach, and then I'll spill some wine on the floor where he will slip and fall and crack his head open.

And if he won't slip on the wine on his own, I'll find a way to crack his head open myself.

Logistics. I have to work out the logistics of the night but I'm getting there. It's all coming together in my head.

Whichever way he dies, I know nobody will ask questions because no one will be there when it happens—that I can count on.

My mother-in-law has no right to request an autopsy or an investigation like Levi's mother did because I am Jordan's wife. Nobody takes importance over the spouse. I am the only person that is allowed to ask questions and request anything. Nobody will care about what Susan thinks even if she tries to argue with me about getting an autopsy.

Unlike when a wife disappears or dies, the husband is the first to be blamed. However, nobody ever doubts the wife when the husband turns up missing or suddenly passes away.

Being a married woman has so many perks, but being a widow will provide a hell of a lot more.

2 9

Another "accidental" murder

My wife has her flaws which annoy the hell out of me. That doesn't mean I will not defend her from her own selfish narcissistic brother though. Especially when he thinks he can take advantage of her.

Mike is a conniving son of a bitch and he will not get away with his antics. This guy has been a burden and an annoyance since the day I met him. Granted, he has only been in my life for a short amount of time, he has still managed to be a royal pain in my ass.

Although Lily can be a pain in my ass too, I still love her. I just don't love *everything* about her anymore. That's why I ended my relationship with Sienna months ago. Dating Sienna for almost a whole year was wrong of me, admittedly, but there are aspects missing from my marriage that I needed from Sienna. And she gave me all of what was missing until I couldn't take her anymore. She, too, started becoming a pain in my ass.

Truly, I do love Lily. I'm just not *in love* with her as much as I was in the beginning of our relationship. After fifteen years of marriage—a total of sharing a life together for sixteen, with the first year dating back to our glory days when we weren't tethered together by a piece of paper, things change. People change. Personalities change. Marriages die. But the love is still there. A part of it is, at least.

You can still love a person and want to carry a life together but not be *in love* with that same person. I could never imagine a life without Lily.

But when Richard introduced me to Sienna, she stole my attention right away. Because she *wanted* my attention. Unlike my wife who hadn't shown any desire for my touch or my company in a long time.

Everything was going great between me and Sienna until I bought her that ridiculously expensive car that she basically bribed me into buying, along with all that extravagant jewelry I've never thought twice about getting for Lily. That's when it dawned on me, Sienna never loved me. She was using me. She had the illusion that I was wealthy, simply because I am a business owner and well, because I told her that I had a lot of money when we first started dating. I lied in the beginning of our relationship to make myself look appealing. I wanted to seem interesting.

Little does she know how much I hate spending money, especially when it feels forced—when an expense is unnecessary. After the car purchase, enough was enough. I had to let her go, no matter how good the sex was. Her gold-digging ways were too much for me to handle and then when I told her our affair was over, *she* was the one who couldn't handle it.

I tried to end our relationship after I bought her that ten-year-old Lexus. Not brand-new like she asked for but expensive enough to keep her satisfied. Except that still didn't work. She still showed up at Richard's party even though she swore she wouldn't because she knew Lily would be there! If she were a man, I would have gotten rid of her by now. But she's a woman. A pathetic gold-digging woman. And unless a woman kills a child (that is my only exception) then I believe women do not deserve to die, no matter how much of a bitch they might be. In Sienna's case, she borders the thin line of deserving death and life. *A very thin line.*

Honestly, I thought about popping over to her apartment to give her a piece of my mind after her little stunt in front of Lily at Richard's party, but I refrained.

After everything I have been faced with during these past few weeks, I need to let my anger out on someone. The perfect person to do that on is Mike. After Lily told me that he guilt-tripped her into giving him rent money, I decided to pay him a visit in Jacksonville. He needs to know he can't get away with using her because she is his sister. I don't want her to have a mental breakdown, given everything that has gone on lately. She isn't strong enough to handle carrying the secret of Levi's death, all while being guilt-tripped for money by her own brother.

She thinks I never knew about her savings account. Correction—I did and I just never cared. Don't most women in relationships have their own bank account that is separate from their spouse? I think it's a good thing. Let her use her own money and not spend any of mine.

See, it is boys like Mike who infuriate me. Boys like him who think they can take advantage of women. Whether they beat on them, guilt-trip them, or are just plain rude to a female, their disgusting actions make me want to get rid of them.

Although I am a cheater, (yes, I know what I am) I am different than boys like Mike and Levi. I did not take advantage of Sienna. She ended up taking advantage of me. I also didn't take advantage of my wife. I just lied to her. That is not nearly as bad as hitting a woman or making a woman pay four thousand dollars for rent that she should not be responsible for.

I pulled up to Mike's apartment just as he was getting in his truck about ten minutes ago. I had no idea where he was going until he drove to a small park. There is a bike path that wraps two miles long around a large lake. He parked in a parallel spot alongside the bridge that overlooks the lake before he got out to open the bed of his truck. He's so oblivious; he didn't notice that I followed him here until I just stepped out of my car.

"Never ask my wife for money ever again. I don't give a fuck that she is your sister. You have some nerve, kid!" I shout while approaching him.

"What the hell? The fuck are you doing here?" Mike huffs as he turns around to see me walking up to him. Looks like he was about to go on a bike ride. For a fucker who is so broke that he can't pay rent, he sure has the time to ride around on a weekday like he has no job.

"You're lucky Lily gave you the money you demanded or else you'd be homeless."

Mike steps back. A smug smile appears on his face. "Like hell I would be."

"I don't know how much of a fuck up you have to be that you can't afford two months of rent but that is not your sister's problem. You should have never asked her for money. You better pay her back."

"She didn't give me any money for rent. Lily never told me to pay her back and she's the one who gave the money to me because the money was *hers*. Not yours. It was *hers*. It came out of her own bank account. So, mine and my sister's arrangement is none of your concern."

"Then what did you need four thousand dollars for if it wasn't for rent?"

"To keep your secrets to myself, but since you're being such an asshole, I am rethinking my decision to stay silent." Mike's smirk makes me want to grab him by the neck and toss him over the bridge.

"What? What secret?" It is a massive challenge to restrain myself. Lily better not have told him about Levi...

"Oh, don't play dumb with me. Hell, you are pretty fucking dumb, but you know what I'm talking about. I know what you did to Levi and to someone else when you were younger. You killed two people. I told Lily I wouldn't go to the police and I normally keep my promises, especially when there is money involved. But hey, I can still pull back on my offer. The money's already mine. I can do whatever the hell I want now."

This smug fucking asshole. I tolerated him longer than I should have. Since he knows my secret, he has to go. I'll deal with my wife later. I knew she wouldn't be able to handle keeping Levi's death to herself. She blabbed to my mother about me talking to the detective on the phone and somehow blabbed to Mike that I killed Levi too.

But wait a second... Mike just said he knows about the other person I killed when I was younger. This means he knows about Jerry except he didn't call him by name. That's the only person I ever got rid of before Levi. Lily doesn't know about Jerry. So then, how does Mike know about him?

"You look like I just broke your brain," Mike laughs. "Remember when I stayed the night and your mom came to chat with you the next morning? I heard everything you guys talked about. I heard about your first victim, your mother's boyfriend."

Shit. I wondered if Mike heard anything my mom said that morning when I found him in my bathroom after she left. I had no idea he was even in my house until I walked in on him. With everything that's been going on lately, particularly the investigation weighing over me, I did not have the time to reflect on Mike overhearing mine and my mother's conversation. *Fuck my life.*

No. Actually, fuck his life. Time for this kid to go. I have had enough of his shit.

"Oh, little Mikey. You should never confront a killer. You never know what we're going to do."

All I need to do is get my hands around his scrawny neck...

But Mike steps back quickly when he says, "You should know to never confront another man either because you never know what he's carrying on him."

Swiftly, Mike pulls a gun out from his waistband. It was hidden beneath his oversized T-shirt so I had no idea he was armed. His movements weren't as fast as he wanted them to be though, which gives me enough time to move forward and grab his arm before he can aim the weapon at me and get his finger on the trigger.

This would be a beneficial time to have my own gun on me. What good is it in my car right now, several feet away? Initially, I bought the damn thing in case I encounter road rage which has happened many times on my drive home from work before. In Miami, aggressive drivers are common. This is Florida after all. Carrying a gun is equally as common as there are road rages. A lot of the times, they go hand in hand.

Now would be the time to whip my gun out of my own waistband, had it been on me like Mike has his, but he beat me to it.

Even though I stopped Mike from aiming the gun at me, my attempt to knock the firearm out of his hands falls short. His grasp remains strong around the pistol grip while struggling underneath me. Our scuffle feels like an eternity when in reality, it only lasts a few seconds before—

BANG.

The noise of the shot distracts me for a brief moment. Not long enough to distract me into letting go of him though. I know I wasn't the one who pulled the trigger. Mike must have blindly wrapped his finger around and pulled it. Thankfully, the shot didn't land on me. Unfortunately, he didn't shoot himself either.

In a desperate attempt to release himself from my grip, he falls against the truck door—his head taking the brunt of the fall as his forehead connects with the top of the driver's door he left open. The gun lands next to my shoes on the pavement. And there goes Mike, unconscious on the ground right next to the gun. Unfortunately, still breathing.

Not for long though. Just as I did with Levi's body on the beach, I grab Mike from underneath the arms and pull him toward the bridge. It's a struggle to lift his body up and over the bridges edge, but I get it done.

There he goes—one hard push and he topples over the bridge; a loud splash echoes the air from the impact of the drop seconds later. I bend down to pick up his gun, frantically looking around for the shell casing from the bullet. I should not leave evidence behind, but I fear there is no time to keep looking for it. I toss his gun over the bridge right after him. Another splash echoes the midday air.

Dragging two dead weight bodies on separate occasions and circumstances recently, have proven to me that it is time to up the weight in my workouts at the gym. If getting rid of two bodies lately has taught me anything, it's that I have been lacking in my strength training.

Now to stage the accident so I can get the hell home and be done with this mess. I have to be quick before someone drives by or even worse, pulls into one of these parallel spots for the park. Thankfully, it is a weekday in the middle of the day so nobody is here. There's a chance someone could arrive at any time though. Time to make his disappearance look like a true tragedy. Conveniently for me, Mike parked his truck in a parallel spot on the side of the road, right against the bridge.

This is a long shot of what I am about to stage but the theory is possible. I have to think quick and this is all I can come up with; An accident. I will make Mike's disappearance look similar to how Jerry and Levi died except this time, there is no alcohol involved. Staging accidents worked two times for me. I can make it work a third.

Mike's truck bed is already unlatched. Instead of pulling out the bicycle from the back as he was planning to do before I showed up, I grab his jack and the tire iron to unscrew the lug nuts on his wheel. Quickly, I jack up the truck near the front driver's side tire. Time to get my pocket knife out of my car.

Man, that would have come in handy if it were in my pocket where it should have been. I could have stabbed him and not worried about overpowering him to get his gun. I wouldn't have to worry about a stray shell casing anywhere either.

You know, after today I will ramp up my own security. No more leaving my weapons in the car. Obviously, I need them with me at all times to defend myself.

With the pocket knife, I rush back over to Mike's truck, stab the tire, then watch the rubber slowly deflate. I unscrew the lug nuts and go as far as taking the tire off the rim. I place it near the spare tire which is sitting right next to the truck on the road.

This is perfect! Now it looks like someone ran him over while changing a tire. Right before he could get the spare on. Maybe it could look like someone hit him while he was walking around to the other side of the vehicle. Yes! That's what I'll do.

I'll move the spare tire in front of the truck, closest to the road where a car would drive by. Then whoever hit him, possibly threw his body in the lake, hence the blood over the bridge. No sense in cleaning it up. Might as well commit to the scene now!

Yes! That works! It has to work. He's already in the water. Time for me to leave. What's done is done.

Another accidental death that does not fall under my responsibility. Just like Levi's and just like that shitty boyfriend my mom dated over two decades ago. All of those guys, excuse me—all of those *boys* because they surely cannot be called men after the way they took advantage of the women in their lives, are now dead in the ground. In Mike's case—in the water, where they each deserve to be. Three less existences in this world. All thanks to me. I've done women a favor.

Now there is nothing else to worry about aside from Sienna. I received my insurance payout, the investigation is closed, and Mike is out of my life for good.

Other than a much needed conversation with my wife about learning to keep her damn mouth shut, Sienna is the last loose end I have to cleanup.

3 0

A w e e k a n d a
h a l f l a t e r

Mike proudly took the money he demanded from me and disappeared last week. It's not like I expected to hear from him again, but it is a little odd that his phone goes straight to voicemail every time I call him. Even though he got what he wanted, he should at least have the decency to answer my calls or texts.

After he took my money, I let four days pass before deciding to contact him. At first, I thought he was just ignoring me on purpose. Then after sending a couple texts which have been left unread and after I tried calling a few more times, I began thinking he blocked my number. I feared he was going to turn me and Jordan into the police about Levi even after he drained my account. What if he didn't keep his word even after manipulating me into giving him all that money?

I attempted to reach out to him a couple times from the phone at work, but I still got his voicemail every single time. I even used an employee's cell phone to try and get ahold of him twice. I still got his voicemail. The phone never even rang. So no, he did not block my phone number. And he damn well has enough money to pay his phone bill, especially after I just gave him four thousand dollars.

If Mike got a new phone number and didn't tell me, then the number I've been calling would have said it was out of service instead of going straight to his voicemail. Something just feels wrong. He's incredibly annoying but he would not just go off the grid like this.

His absence would not normally inflict worry in me but given the circumstances of our interactions lately, things have changed. Even though he blackmailed me, my instincts tell me he might be in trouble. No matter how much Mike irritates me, tries to steal my car, extorts me for money and God knows what else, I still care about him.

When my phone buzzes in my pocket, I rush out of the dining room at work where I had just been dealing with a customer complaint regarding one of my servers, and into the kitchen to see who's calling.

An unrecognizable number appears on my phone. Is this Mike? Did he somehow read my mind and he knows that I'm thinking about him? Are we somehow connected through sibling telepathy?

No. Unfortunately, I'm wrong. Instead of Mike, an authoritative unrecognizable voice answers my hello. "Can I speak with Lily Hoffman?"

"This is her. Who's calling?"

"This is Detective Shareen. Ma'am, I am calling you about Michael Wallace. His truck was found parked in Waterfront Park in

Jacksonville, Florida. The driver's side door was left open, but the owner of the vehicle, Michael, is nowhere to be found. His wallet was left in the truck. It looks like he was changing a tire off the side of the road and never finished. Your name came up as his closest relative. Is that correct?"

Well talk about sibling telepathy after all.

"Uh, yes. I'm his sister," I manage to say, my heart beginning to thud rapidly. What is she about to tell me? What is this panic that is suddenly engulfing my heavy chest?

"Have you spoken to your brother lately, ma'am?"

"Not for a few days now, no. I've been calling and texting but he hasn't answered. When... when did you find his truck at the park?"

"Someone reported an abandoned truck at Waterfront Park yesterday. According to the address on your brother's license, the park is about a ten-minute drive from his apartment. I am not sure how long his vehicle was parked there before the caller reported it though."

"Was... was his phone in his truck? Every time I call him, I keep getting his voicemail."

"No, Ma'am. We did not find a phone anywhere in the vehicle. His wallet was left in the glove compartment, that was all. If I may suggest, you should file a missing persons police report with us. If I'm being honest, the scene looks like he may have been hit by another vehicle or fallen off the side of the bridge when he was changing his tire. I can't rule out a hit and run accident or confirm whether he fell over the bridge or exactly what happened yet. I am only speculating, given the circumstances. There is no evidence of any marks or dents on his vehicle, so if someone *did* hit into him, it looks like they didn't strike his truck. They might've only struck him. Anything is possible. I can't rule out any possibility until you report him missing. Then I can further investigate the scene."

"Is... can you..." I can't form a proper sentence as my thoughts override my response. *A hit and run. Fell over the bridge. How would he fall off the bridge while changing a tire?*

This has to be Jordan's fault. There is no way this is a coincidence. Nothing is a coincidence as long as my cheating husband is involved. He was gone all day and into the night only two days after he found the money in my purse—two days after Mike met me at my job and took the four thousand. Jordan said he was doing inventory on the moving equipment when he stayed at work late that night. He didn't come home until midnight. That was a week ago, right when I stopped hearing from Mike.

I did not bother to believe Jordan or question where he actually was because who the fuck cares anymore! He was probably with that Sienna/Sharon slut, I had thought. There is no point in caring about what he tells me anymore since I know he is a cheating lying bastard. Now... now I have an inkling as to where he really was.

"Can you get a search team or something?" is all I can manage to get out over the phone to the detective.

"Yes, ma'am. We can arrange that. I needed to contact you first because you have to report your brother as a missing person in order for me to get a search team going."

"Okay. Yes, please," I say.

"Can you come into the station to make an official report? I'll get a search team out at the lake tomorrow morning once that's done."

"Tomorrow? What about today?"

"It will take a couple hours to get a team together after the report is filed. By that time, it will be sundown tonight. Better to search for your brother in the daylight, bright and early tomorrow."

After the short amount of time Mike and I have spent together—after all the stress and irritation he has caused me, fear is not the first emotion I thought would hit me when I would hear something bad could have happened...

After I end the call with the detective, I make a split decision to clock out at work. I tell my employees to hold down the restaurant without me for the day, then I text my higher ups about another family emergency. And this time, sadly, my emergency regarding my brother is actually real.

In my car, I make my way toward I-95 and head to Jacksonville. I could have chosen to file the missing persons report over the phone with that detective except I want to do some in person investigating myself. So, I might as well file the report when I get there. Also, it won't matter whether I make the report on the phone right now or in a few hours because she said the team won't search the lake until tomorrow morning anyway. It's a little after three o'clock in the afternoon. By the time I get there, the sun will be already done setting.

Five and a half hours later, thanks to all the traffic, I arrive at the police station and file a report. It doesn't take as long as I expected it would.

The search team is scheduled to show up right at sunrise tomorrow morning. Since I am in town and now without plans to go back home until after the search, this is a perfect time to utilize the apartment key Mike exchanged with me when I gave him my house key.

With a sliver of hope that he might be inside of his apartment, I knock three times before entering.

There is no answer so I let myself in with the key I have never used before.

A strong horrible stench hits me as soon as the door opens. By the smell, the sight of the flies buzzing around the trashcan, and the disarray of dishes left soaked in water in the sink, it is obvious Mike hasn't been home in *days*. Immediately, I take out the trash to get rid of the smell before rummaging around the place for his phone, but there's nothing to find in here.

I should talk to a neighbor or get in touch with his landlord to see when or if anyone has spoken and seen him last.

Nobody answers next door when I knock three times, so I move on to knock on the door that's on the other side of Mike's apartment. A woman who looks to be around my age, wearing black sweatpants and a blue baggy college T-shirt, answers the door.

"Hi, sorry to bother you. I'm your next-door neighbor's sister. Mike hasn't been answering my calls and I'm kind of worried about him. Have you heard from or seen him lately?"

"Oh, I haven't seen him in about a week," she responds. "His truck hasn't been here either. You know, I did notice another car follow him when he left to go on a bike ride the last time I saw him."

"What color was it?" I ask.

"A black sedan. I think it was a Toyota. He was parked a few spots over, never got out, then pulled out after Mike did."

My husband owns a black Toyota Camry. As I said, nothing is a coincidence when he is involved.

Detective Shareen told me Mike's truck is still parked at the lake and won't get towed yet since the area might be classified as a crime scene, depending on what happens tomorrow during the search. Before settling into his apartment for the night, I'm going to head to the park to investigate the area myself. Not sure why I need to see it. Something just tells me I should look now before anyone from the search team arrives tomorrow.

Ten minutes later, my GPS takes me to Waterfront Park. Mike's truck is parked in a parallel spot next to the bridge overlooking the lake. The driver's side is jacked up and the wheel is missing. It looks like he was in the middle of changing his tire just as the detective mentioned on the phone. Is it really possible that someone ran him off the road? There's nobody here and it's not like the park is in the middle of a high traffic area.

Did Jordan do this... like my intuition is telling me? After all, I ended up being right about him cheating. I shouldn't second guess myself now. Not especially after that woman just told me she saw a vehicle suspiciously follow Mike in the same make and color car as my husband's.

On the off chance that Jordan wasn't behind this, then was somebody else after Mike? Maybe it was someone who wanted the money Mike blackmailed me for. There must've been a reason he demanded the four thousand dollars in cash only. Was it to pay someone off—someone who took the four thousand then killed him after? They could have made his disappearance look like an accident.

An accident...

No, I should not second guess myself. Staging an accident is just my husband's style of getting rid of a person.

Time to corroborate where Jordan really was the night he told me he stayed late at work. I happen to have Richard's number because Jordan used my phone when his had to get fixed a few years ago. Jordan needed to get in contact with both Richard and Levi, so he used mine for a few days. Thankfully, I never deleted Richard's number out of my contacts.

"Richard? Hi, it's Lily. Was my husband at work every day last week? Did he stay really late one night with you to go over inventory? Or did he leave early one day?" I have no time for small talk. My anxiety is taking over. My words fly out of my mouth. The phone shakes in my trembling hands while my feet pace back and forth in front of Mike's truck.

"Oh, uh..." Richard stutters. I have clearly taken him off guard which is what I wanted to do.

"Please, just answer me. It's important," I say, unexpectedly on the verge of frustrated tears. "I won't tell him I talked to you. Please, I just need answers."

"Well, Jordan was at work every day, but we never stayed late to do inventory together. Uh..." There is a spark of concern in his voice. He's conflicted.

"Uh, what? Do you have something else to tell me, Richard?"

"Listen, you sound like something is going on between you two, so I'll just let you know that he left early once last week. He left sometime around noon, I think. He said he had a doctor's appointment."

Well, that is most certainly not true. Jordan never had a doctor's appointment because I make our appointments.

"Which day did he leave for his appointment?" I grit my teeth.

"Maybe Monday or Tuesday. I can't really remember, sorry."

Good enough. No need to continue questioning Richard. He obviously felt uncomfortable just now. At the same time, it was also obvious he didn't have an issue talking to me about Jordan. In fact, he volunteered information that implicated Jordan. Why would another man—someone who is supposed to be a best friend and business partner choose not to blatantly cover for his buddy? It's obvious why I called. I'm suspicious of my husband. It's all in my tone of voice.

I bet Richard knows about Jordan's affair. He probably wants me to know about it too, but didn't want to directly tell me. He thinks my question pertained to my husband having an affair, not him being a killer.

Jordan got home around midnight last week. If he drove to Jacksonville at noon, then yes, he would have got back home at midnight.

As history goes, I should follow where my instincts and evidence lead me. And they're leading me toward believing Jordan made Mike disappear, which means my little brother's disappearance inadvertently ended up being all my fault.

Oh, how I can't wait to be a widow soon!

31

Two can play at that game

After almost six long hours, the search team found Mike's body in the lake. I actually cried when they pulled him out of the water and I had to identify him to the officer. As the detective told me, she believes an altercation ensued or someone accidentally hit him, then dumped him in the water before driving away. It's all speculation because there are no security cameras in the park and no key witnesses that they know of to confirm what truly happened.

I know her speculation is only partially correct though. Nothing is truly ever a coincidence in this world. Everything connects in some way or another. And Jordan is the connector in this situation. The police are right about someone dumping Mike into the water. That person had to have been Jordan. I doubt he crashed into Mike though because he wouldn't have caused unnecessary damage to his car, which would lead to unnecessary expenses to fix. As much as I don't know my husband, I do know how he thinks when it comes to murder. I know exactly how experienced he is in making murders look like accidents.

I believe Jordan left work early the day Richard told me he did and instead of going to a doctor appointment, he drove here to see Mike. Whatever happened between them, sadly led to the death of my little brother.

The night before the scheduled search, I slept in Mike's place alone, dreading what was to come the following morning. After I cleaned up his apartment because I couldn't stand the stench in the place and the sight of the maggots in the garbage can, I looked through every inch of his belongings. There were no signs of anyone potentially blackmailing him like he did to me. Nothing raised any red flags on his social media which was conveniently logged in on his computer, so I could snoop through his messages. No shady conversations or emails. And then I found the money I gave him. The entire four thousand dollars was still rolled up in rubber bands hidden in a drawer.

He didn't even get to use the money yet. If he was being blackmailed or owed some kind of debt to anyone, he wouldn't have let a week go by without paying the person back. That would not make any sense. I have no idea what he needed the money for, whether four thousand was just a random number he manipulated me into giving him or if there was a true reason for it, but I can rule out anyone else, other than my husband as a suspect in his murder.

I left Jacksonville yesterday and got home around midnight last night. Once I got home, I told Jordan the search team found my brother's body in a lake and that's where I was all day. When he heard me tell him where the search team found Mike dead, he didn't look the least bit panicked at what I said. I didn't bother to tell him that the police won't look very hard into Mike's death though. Instead, I lied and told him they're going to check a security camera in the park. Little does he know, the camera is nonexistent.

Let this man fucking squirm in silence. Let him live the last few days of his life worrying, in fear. Although the fear isn't written on Jordan's face—deep down, I assume he must be panicking.

Or he might just be such a psychopath that he isn't worried about getting caught at all.

Speaking of Jordan's upcoming death, it's time to get answers to my Sharon/Sienna question before I kill him. I can't ask him directly, but I have other ways to get my answers. And the only person who can answer whether Sharon and Sienna are the same person, is Richard. I know Sienna exists because we met in person. What I don't know is whether her real name is Sharon or Sienna.

Jordan said Sienna is Richard's friend. Since Richard willingly told me that my husband left work early last week over the phone, he should answer me when I ask him about Jordan's mistress. Well, I will not flat out say the word *mistress* when I ask about the bitch, but my point will get across.

Time for an impromptu visit at their workplace.

The chime from the bell on top of the glass door dings, alerting Jordan of my arrival.

"Honey? Oh, hi. What are you doing here?" Jordan looks up from his desk in shock. *No way in hell Lily's here,* he must be thinking. Rightfully so, his shocked state of mind is valid. Never once have I ever come here for any reason unannounced. Or announced for that matter.

"Surprise! Surprise!" I smile brightly while setting a large pizza box on top of his desk. "I wanted to drop you off some lunch for once."

"Oh, how nice of you. You never do this." Jordan exchanges an odd look at the box, then at me.

"That's why I said *for once*," I smirk. It is a massive challenge to hide my disdain and frustration with this man. Richard isn't at his desk which is only a few feet in front of Jordan's. Richard's car was parked outside though, so he has to be in this small building somewhere. Although this place isn't big, the back parking lot is of good size since it is full of ten moving trucks. For a small moving company, they do pretty well, honestly. Richard must be somewhere outside near the trucks since he isn't in here.

"Today's my day off so I figured it'd be nice to stop by. I had a craving for pizza and the place I went to only sold a whole pie so I brought you guys the rest of it. I already had two slices. Couldn't eat the whole thing all by myself."

"Hell, you know I could," Jordan huffs, reaching for a slice of pepperoni, his favorite.

"There's plenty for Richard if he wants some. Where is he?"

"He went out back to help one of our movers with a truck. Engine light was on or something— Oh, never mind." Jordan chews the pizza loudly as he gestures at the door behind me. The bells chime as it swings open and in walks Richard.

Oh good, what perfect timing. Now time to figure out how I can get him alone with me and how to convince my husband to leave the office.

"Hey, man. Lily brought us some pizza," Jordan says to Richard.

"Oh, thanks! I'm starving. Was just about to go pick up some lunch in an hour," Richard says.

"Well now you don't need to anymore," I gesture toward the open box. "Help yourself."

Jordan's cell phone vibrates against his desk and that prompts an idea out of me.

After looking through my purse and praying that my phone won't ring while I search for nothing, I let out a dramatic sigh. "Oh, shit. I must have left my phone in the car. Honey, would you mind going to get it for me? There was a homeless guy on the road right outside of the building when I got here. He was eyeing me when I got out. He tried to get my attention but I ignored him. I don't really want to deal with him again. And if my phone is sitting on the seat, I don't want him breaking the window trying to get it."

Jordan swallows the hefty bite of his pizza slice and rolls his eyes. It's apparent he doesn't want to get up from his seat, let alone do anything for me, but he has to oblige because he was just asked to do a favor for his own wife in front of another man. A man wouldn't say no to his wife in front of another man because that would make him look bad. On the contrary theory of what is perceived, men *do* care what others think. Just depends on the context and situation. And who the other person is.

Once Jordan's out of the office and out of sight, there is no time to waste.

"Richard, have you ever met Levi's ex-girlfriend? I think her name was Sharon or Sienna?"

"Sharon," Richard nods. He's avoiding eye contact. That tells me he must know something about the affair. "Sienna is a friend of mine. You might have met her at my party."

Oh, yes. Indeed, I did meet the bitch.

"Yeah, I met Sienna but not Sharon. Actually, I didn't even know Levi had a girlfriend. Were you friends with her?"

"Me and Sharon? Oh no. Not at all. I met her twice. She was uh, a bit toxic from what Levi shared. You know, me and Gia were talking about Levi the other day and we were wondering how Sharon was holding up," he says.

So then Sharon isn't Sienna. Sharon *is* a real person who I've never met and the toxic relationship Jordan told me about is true.

But whether Jordan justified killing Levi because he was the abuser and Sharon might not have played a role in the toxicity (I'm not trying to victim blame but some victims aren't entirely always one hundred percent innocent), Jordan still deserves death himself. For cheating, lying, spending our money, putting me in debt, and killing a person prior to getting in a relationship with me without disclosing his past.

"Wait, so you did meet Sienna?" Richard raises his eyebrows.

That's the look. He knows my husband is a cheating two-timing son of a bitch.

But before I can answer him, the click of the front door sounds in the distance. My husband is going to walk in here and say he can't find my phone because it has been in my purse all along. Time to wrap this up before it rings and gives me away. Even though it's clear that Richard knows about Sienna, he is still an innocent bystander in this situation. Jordan is the one who needs to die.

The bell chimes on top of the door to the office. In walks my two-timing husband. "Honey, I didn't find your phone on the seat." Jordan sighs. "Are you sure you left it in the car?"

He's irritated that he had to walk out in the heat for me. If only he burned in hell under the sweltering sun while he was out there.

"Well, it isn't in my purse," I say while making another fake attempt to peek through my things. "It's okay though. It probably fell in between the car seat. I was just about to leave anyway. I didn't realize the time. Don't want to get caught in lunch rush hour traffic. I'll look for it myself. Enjoy the pizza, guys."

I hope Richard enjoys his pizza. Jordan can choke on it.

3 2

Get rid of, Get rid of

The payout from the insurance company came in which means I can finally get Sienna out of my life once and for all. Even though getting rid of Sienna's existence would be a much easier and cheaper option for me, paying her off will have to do. Money will keep the gold digger out of my life forever. All she wanted was my money before, so now that is what she's going to get.

I know this is my karma for having an affair. This is my fault for letting things get out of hand. I admit it, but now I am working on redeeming myself.

I grab my ungodly expensive iPhone that I regret purchasing out of my nightstand drawer. That was my first mistake in mine and Sienna's relationship. I made her think I like extravagant and luxurious things. Using a cheap burner phone would have been less expensive and easier on my end when it came to keeping up communication with her, except I had to make myself look the part of being a wealthy man. That included owning the latest version of whatever the fuck number iPhone this is. My daily regular cell phone is a basic android. It takes pictures, connects to the internet, has storage, makes calls and sends texts. That's all I need—simplicity.

But Sienna needed more.

She always, always needed more from me, no matter what the hell it was. She was never satisfied with anything.

The sex was great; that I will miss. It is not worth the mental stress and money that has accumulated and come out of my pocket over the past few months though. Even before Lily accused me of cheating with Gia when we were in the Keys, I had already decided my affair with Sienna was over. I thought my wife caught me that day on the beach until she said she suspected Gia was my mistress. I dodged a bullet that day.

Well, technically, Gia dodged Lily's bullet.

When Lily told me she would work through things with me, I knew I didn't have to worry about Sienna anymore. Even if Lily finds out about my real affair, she'll forgive me. She said it herself.

I unlock my phone and open my conversation with Sienna to send her my last text. This is the last time I will ever contact her on this phone, then I'm returning it, and getting my money back.

I said I had one last surprise but I was wrong. When you showed up at Richard's party, I knew what you were doing. How about twenty thousand dollars to get you out of my life for good? That's enough to move

to the Bahamas as you've always wanted. I'll cover the fee to import your brand-new car there too. I told you our affair is over and I meant it.

Reply from S: Thirty thousand and you'll never hear from me again.

I knew she would ask for more money which is why I lowballed her first. This way, the remaining money out of the fifty-thousand that I received from the insurance payout will go toward paying off the car loan for Sienna's fancy car, the import fee as I just stated, and then toward my credit card debt that I racked up during our secret dates. That leaves only a little bit left for me to put in savings. But hey, a little is better than nothing. All my mistakes are about to be righted.

I text her back—

Perfect. Meet me at our spot Saturday night. 8 pm.

She doesn't text back. Instead, she only sends a thumbs up reaction to the message.

Tomorrow better be the last time I ever see and hear from Sienna again. If not, then I really may have to rethink my oath to not kill a woman. I'll have no other choice but to get rid of her if this doesn't remove her from my life.

3 3

Retaliation day

Retaliation day is here. Jordan will soon endure the proper payback for all the lies he has told me and the death he is responsible for, especially for my little brother's death. And especially for not only cheating on me once, but having a repeated affair! That's what really gets me angry. He betrayed our marriage over and over again.

I have no idea how many times Jordan and that bitch were physically intimate, but the conversations on his secret phone were enough to prove it was a full-on affair. Hell, their affair could still be going on for all I know. The last few text messages between the two of them on his secret phone insinuated that Jordan ended things between them, but who the fuck knows what's really going on at this point?

Regardless of what was or still is, Jordan is going to pay the price for being unfaithful to me. And he will pay that price tonight.

When I initially thought he was just cheating with Gia, I thought we could get past his unfaithfulness. Oh, but I no longer think that way anymore though! Not after everything I have learned. The lies. The debt.

The car. The other woman. The people he's killed, especially my own brother.

The time for retaliation is now. It's a perfect night to break out the wine in celebration of the payout Jordan got from the life insurance policy. I have gone over my plan several times. I even rehearsed how frantic I need to make my voice sound when I call the police tonight. I'm ready for this.

Phase one of my plan is done. We just got home from our dinner which was surprisingly good. The price of our dinner nearly killed Jordan which made me internally laugh when he saw the bill. Oh, imagine if he died right there at the table!

Now on to phase two of the night.

While heading to the refrigerator to grab a pre-chilled chardonnay bottle, I set the music to play over our Bluetooth speakers in the living room and turn the volume all the way up. The music is so loud that we have to nearly yell to hear each other. Jordan strikes me an odd look when the volume nearly reaches its limits.

"What's wrong? You don't like the music?" I shout in response to his judgemental look at the volume. "We're celebrating!" I dance my way over to him with the wine glasses. I hand him one, then pull him up from the couch, forcing him to get up and dance around the living room with me. His reluctance to move makes me want to slap him.

"Chug! Chug!" Excitedly, I challenge him to finish off the glass before knocking back my own drink. He smiles, rolls his eyes, and begins awkwardly dancing with me.

I can't remember the last time we've done this; dance together. If we've ever even shared a dance together during our fifteen years of marriage. We never even danced during our wedding or honeymoon stage, not that there really was one. After a year of being together, we decided it was time to get married, went to the courthouse, had a celebration with Jordan's mom and our college friends days later, and that was that. There was never a proposal. He never got down on one knee. We never even went on a real honeymoon.

Maybe our marriage was over before it ever even began.

But something ignites in me tonight—in us, for a brief amount of time as we celebrate and soon, we're finishing off the first bottle of Chardonnay. I feel happy... and Jordan looks happy too. The money might be playing a role in his happiness though. Not sure whether it's my company or not. Not even sure if it's *his* company that is making me smile. My emotions could be forming because of the anticipation of what's to come tonight.

A couple glasses of Chardonnay won't get him drunk. However, the right amount of tequila will. Once he takes one shot, he'll end up wanting more. That is, when he isn't planning a murder. I must say, I was surprised when he stayed sober enough to kill Levi in Islamorada. Then again, he thoroughly thought out everything he planned to do that night, so being sober was in the plan. Just like I planned to stay sober enough for tonight.

"Shots?" I run into the kitchen to grab the tequila bottle; his preferred choice of liquor.

Of course, he doesn't deny my offer.

He doesn't even bother to notice I haven't taken any shots myself and that I poured three for him. He shoots back one after another. After tonight, I never want to see a tequila bottle again. I never want to see or touch anything that reminds me of this man after he's dead. Especially that fallen wedding picture neither of us have bothered to pick back up off the ground.

The photo, weighing nearly ten pounds because of its ridiculous thick antique frame I was desperate to buy so many years ago, still lays flat on the beige carpet from when it fell the other day. The black frame matches the black and white shot of us kissing. We didn't actually take the photo at our wedding since we went to the courthouse and had a small get-together after. Instead, I hired a photographer to take candid shots days later. We look so happy and young, which we were, but that photo is no more than a distant memory in our twenties—when we had a beautiful life together that no longer exists.

Three tequila shots later and two full bottles of Chardonnay down, Jordan begins wobbling all over the living room. He can barely keep his eyes open when it starts to happen. My moment is finally here!

Jordan collapses right onto the couch, his eyes rolling back, ready to pass out asleep. He is so inebriated that he can barely stay awake and keep his head upright. I lower the music to be able to focus better. His attempt to speak falls short as his words come out as an incoherent mumble. This is perfect.

Jordan is paralyzed against the couch cushion, aided by the alcohol. He doesn't even notice when I lift our heavy wedding photo and move toward him.

One swift swing up against his chin... and there he goes! His head flies back, landing against the back rest of the couch. Blood pours out of his mouth, down his neck, and plasters the photo frame.

He never even had a chance to open his eyes.

But damn... there's *so* much blood.

I swung the picture frame much stronger than I anticipated. Blood is splattered all over my beautiful navy blue leather couch, red drips from his chin... and oh shit! His tooth—no his *teeth* are knocked out too! I knocked both of his front teeth out!

This is a much messier scene than anticipated. I need to get Jordan off my couch and move him on the ground near the table before more of his blood gets everywhere. The blood can't keep dripping all over the leather or else my idea to make his death look like an accident won't make sense to the police.

This does not look like he fell and knocked himself unconscious...

How can I fix this?

If only Jordan was still alive to give me some pointers.

With immense struggling, I grab his shoulders and pull him toward me. His heavy body instantly falls off the couch due to gravity and my weakness. He lands on my beige carpet, head first, right at my feet, next to my coffee table.

I'm about to smear some of his blood on the edge of the table to make it look like that is what he fell on... but wait, what do I do about the wedding picture?

There's blood all over it!

Okay, I gotta relax. I should be able to just wipe it off.

I rush over to the kitchen to grab a towel, run water over the cloth, then rush back into the living room.

Oh no... no... no... no! My footprints! I just tracked blood into my damn kitchen. Now I have to clean the floor up before the police get here...

Okay, *relax*. I'm panicking. I'm moving too quick. Got to focus on getting this frame clean before calling the police.

I'm scrubbing and scrubbing. The blood is coming off the photo, but not to the extent that it looks squeaky clean... and the more I scrub, a crack in the frame reveals itself. A large crack right on the bottom where it connected with Jordan's chin.

Shit. Shit. Shit.

Getting rid of the picture is not an option either because those two detectives who questioned Jordan about Levi were in my living room. I heard them comment on it to Jordan when I was upstairs. They probably won't be the ones to come back here after I call 9-1-1 tonight, but every inch of this place will most likely be photographed and taken note of... Then those detectives will realize it's gone. That would definitely look suspicious if they notice that the photo is not here anymore, right around the same night my husband dies!

Relax. Breathe.

Jordan was calm when he killed Levi. He was prepared for the aftermath of things and so am I.

I prepared in case things went wrong which they are. My plan A is not working in the way I expected it to. On to plan B.

I didn't want to result to my backup plan, but there is no other choice. If anything I've learned over the past few months it's to always be prepared and to think things through. I need to always be ready for the outcome of my choices. That's why I have a backup plan. And as much as I didn't want to use it, now it is my only option.

34

S i e n n a

It's past eight o'clock at night already. *Where the hell is Jordan?* He said he would be here with my money by now. I know I shouldn't be shocked at his tardiness since he is usually fifteen to twenty minutes late every time we meet up, but my impatience is taking over tonight. It's 8:17 p.m. Where the hell is he? I want the money he promised me. Though his handsome features normally make up for always being late, his looks do not excuse his actions tonight. Tonight, I overlook his muscular arms, six pack of abs, and perfectly trimmed beard.

When the entrance opens in the bar, I expect Jordan to walk in. Instead, two police officers enter. Nobody has been loud or acted rowdy as long as I've been here so it's a bit strange to see the police here.

One of them just locked eyes with me.

Wait... why are they walking toward me?

I look over my shoulder. Maybe they're looking at someone behind me...

"Sienna Murphy," one of the uniformed cops boasts my full name as they approach my table.

What the fuck? I turn around slowly to see the uniformed men hovering over my table.

"Um, yes? What can I help you with?" I ask without willing to get up. This must be a mistake. How did they know to look for me here? And what the hell would they want from me?

"Sienna Murphy, you're under arrest for the murder of Jordan Hoffman."

"What?" I shout in disbelief. *Jordan's dead? How? This makes no sense.* "I-I-I didn't kill him, I swear! When did he die? I-I-I just spoke to him yesterday. We were supposed to meet right now. I-I-I didn't murder him, I swear! You have the wrong person."

"Miss Murphy, we have video evidence that you were the last person at Jordan Hoffman's house before he was found dead late last night. There are also text messages between you two that suggests of an affair and confirmation that he invited you over last night, to which you agreed and arrived."

Oh, my god.

I knew something was wrong when I showed up to his house. Jordan must have set me up... Actually, no. *His wife* must've been the one to set me up!

"I did go to his house, but no one was home. He invited me over through text—yes, that's true, but he wasn't there. The door was unlocked, so I let myself in. I thought he left it unlocked for me, but then I realized he wasn't home. I left only a few minutes later.

Officer, I didn't kill him. I swear! His wife must've set me up! It was her, it had to be!"

"A few minutes is all it takes to commit a murder, ma'am. You're under arrest for the murder of Jordan Hoffman..."

I can't believe this. The last time I saw Jordan was here in this bar during Richard's surprise party, but that was weeks ago. Our last interaction in person was when Jordan hastily acted like he forgot about my existence in front of Lily. We only spoke on the phone once afterward. He called to tell me how angry he was with me for introducing myself to her.

Then he texted me yesterday morning, asking to meet him here tonight at the bar. I agreed before he texted me once more, for the final time last night when he invited me over his house. It was around eight o'clock when he told me he was dying to see me and didn't want to wait to meet at the bar anymore. When I showed up at his house, I thought it was strange he wasn't there so I tried calling him. When he didn't answer the phone, I just figured we would still meet here tonight at the bar like we originally planned. I figured something must've happened since nobody was home. I should have never walked in... but Lily's car was gone so I thought he was alone.

But it all makes sense now. She probably found out about us and either made him text me last night or got her hands on his secret phone. I was ignorant to the fact that he was married in the beginning of our relationship, but in other aspects, I knew when he was lying to me. Jordan thought I didn't know that iPhone he flaunted was only to put on a show for me. It was obvious by how brand new it looked and how he handled it with careful intention that it was all to keep up the illusion that he was wealthy. Nobody ever called or texted him on that phone while he was with me. In fact, they always called him on his other phone—*his piece of shit android work phone* as he would always call it.

Jordan created the illusion that he had a lot of money and I realized that shortly after we started dating. I knew the moving company couldn't have been the reason he was supposedly so wealthy because Richard was my long-time friend. The business didn't rake in enough money to match Jordan's lifestyle. He said he made most of his money in the stock market. He said running the business with Richard and Levi was just for fun. And I believed him until I realized it was all of façade. Until Richard told me he had a wife.

But I still stayed with Jordan even after I knew that. Regardless of how much money he did not have, I couldn't let him go. Everything was fine between us until he broke up with me out of nowhere and acted like I did not exist anymore.

The night we spoke at Richard's party did him in. Jordan was pissed when I spoke to his wife in the bar but I had to! The opportunity was right in front of me. I had to take it. When he bought my car and told me he never wanted to see me again about a month before the party, I warned him that he would regret breaking up with me. That's why I walked right up to him and Lily at the party, knowing exactly who she was. Knowing exactly how Jordan would react when I shook his wife's hand.

But that's his fault for bringing her in the same room as me though! He is the one who cheated on his wife! I am not the reason for their failed marriage. He was. Jordan was the one who made the decision to befriend me after the guys moved my stuff in when they opened their moving company, and he didn't stop there at wanting to be my friend. He continued to flirt through text, and call me late at night before building the courage to ask me out on dates.

Suddenly, the cold clasp of metal around my wrists brings me back to reality. I can't believe these officers are accusing me of his murder. They're really about to send me to jail...

What do I do? How do I get them to believe me that I'm innocent?

I thought I would never see Jordan after taking his money tonight except that was only partially true.

Tears involuntarily escape my eyes. I can't help but think of the mistake I made staying with him...

What a price both of us are paying for having our affair.

An ironic twist

My plan is almost complete. All it took was a simple text message from Jordan on his secret iPhone to his secret bitch, and the home wrecking whore took the bait. She really thought he invited her over and her dumbass showed up. She didn't even ask for my address when "Jordan" texted her, which means she already knew where I live!

She's been in my house before!

They had an affair in my *own* house!

If I hadn't killed Jordan already, he would have been dead soon after I came upon that realization.

Now that things are over and settled, I've reflected on how I could have handled this situation better. Before my suspicions were aimed toward Gia being Jordan's mistress, I never checked the front door camera footage. My assumption and decisions were based off rage and nothing factual. If my emotions never clouded my judgment, I would have had the sense to check the camera and nailed his ass in the act way sooner. Jordan would have been caught in his affair red-handed with the right bitch instead, Sienna. If our cameras didn't delete the footage after two weeks, I'd be able to look back and see the home wrecking whore walk through my door, but too late now.

In the end, everything worked out though. I still got my revenge. Framing Sienna for Jordan's murder was not my first choice because I thought that would cause more problems for me. Still, I made sure to cover my ass just in case things went wrong and thankfully, I did!

Before we left for our celebratory dinner, I walked out of the house with my purse alone to make it look like Jordan was left home alone. I made sure to walk right under the view of the front door camera. That way, the police would see me leave alone when they play back the footage to start investigating the scene of the crime. Then I went back inside through the backdoor and convinced us to leave for dinner through there. That way, the camera never saw us together at all.

At dinner, I took his iPhone and went to the bathroom and texted Sienna to come over. Jordan is such an idiot, he had no idea his iPhone was in my purse the whole night.

It was risky inviting the home wrecking bitch over while we were at dinner because I couldn't stop the camera notification from showing up on Jordan's regular phone. Thankfully, I caught a glimpse of the notification when it appeared on mine just in time. I made sure to distract him from looking at his phone while I watched her walk in and out of the house on mine.

Truthfully, as much as the bitch deserves to rot in prison for the rest of her life, framing her for his murder didn't seem sufficient enough punishment. I wanted her to suffer in silence instead. My backup plan became my only option though. When I killed Jordan and the photo frame was cracked, it became obvious I was staring at the perfect crime scene to frame a mistress. Two empty bottles of wine sitting near his dead body during a late night affair while the wife was away. Our wedding picture as the murder weapon: the perfect outlet for her rage—almost sentimental and poetic.

Instead of making Jordan's death look like an accident—an inadvertent suicide, I blamed his side bitch. When the police showed up after my frantic call, I showed them his iPhone messages, which showed his invite to her only twenty minutes before she arrived. Then I followed up with showing them my doorbell camera recordings. They didn't ask to see me leave the house because all they cared about was spotting the moment Sienna walked in and out of my home. And I made sure to convince Jordan to walk back in the house through the backdoor when we got home from dinner. There was never any footage of him leaving the house that night at all.

The detective just gave me a call, notifying me the murderer—Sienna's home wrecking ass, was arrested.

Now on to the final phase; convincing my mother-in-law into believing I was blindsided by her son's unfaithfulness before she tries to cause problems in my life by asking me unnecessary questions. If I had stuck with my original idea to make Jordan look like he died by hitting his head, she wouldn't have known about her son's infidelity. Now it's time to make her think I never knew about the affair. She needs to know how upset I was. Just not upset enough to kill him. Let's see if she believes me.

Susan opens the front door of her apartment, already bawling her eyes out. This is my cue to let the fake tears trickle down my cheeks too. Pretending to be sad in front of the cops while in the presence of Jordan's lifeless body was much easier than it is to stand in front of my mother-in-law. That was partly because I knew my acting skills had to be top tier at the scene of the crime. The police needed to know I wasn't guilty. I was a shocked and betrayed wife who came home to a gruesome scene; my beloved husband murdered by his mistress who I had no idea existed.

Now I just need to tolerate Susan's presence in my life for about another three weeks or so before I can file a claim with the insurance company to get my money, and then I'll get the fuck out of Miami. The only thing I will miss about this city is the beach. But then again, I can't recall the last time I went to the beach so what is there to miss when I haven't even enjoyed it?

I said I had no desire to ever step foot in New York ever again, but with the right amount of money, I can picture myself living there comfortably. And over a hundred thousand dollars will do just that. Screw the weather. As long as I have a fat checking account, who cares about the cold when I can just keep myself holed up in a nice condo and order food and wine to my door every day?

Maybe I won't even stay in New York for long. Maybe I'll travel the country. I will figure it all out eventually once I receive the insurance payout. Until then, I have to play the role of the grieving betrayed widow here in Miami. And I have to play the part right, beginning with Jordan's mother.

She needs to believe I am as heartbroken about Jordan's murder as she is. Actually, I should be the one to act more heartbroken than she is. As the wife should be.

Honestly, faking my emotions is not really that hard because I am emotional about Jordan's death. Sadness is not the driving force of my feelings though. Anger and relief is. Anger that I had to kill him because of his own choices. Anger toward him for being such a lying cheating asshole. And then there is a small bit of grief for the life we lived before he had his affair—for the time we briefly were in love, and then relief that I am set free from his lies.

Susan goes in for a tight hug, wrapping her frail arms around my shoulders; the wetness of her tears trickles down my skin. I fight the urge to snub her off me.

"Come in, come in," Susan sniffles. "I just made us some coffee."

"Oh, I definitely need it," I sigh and wipe the forced tears out of my eyes. "Haven't slept since... well—I haven't slept for a few days now since it happened."

Hell, if she only knew I've had the best sleep I've ever had in years. The first night was a little rough though. Truly, I didn't get any sleep at all because the adrenaline from taking my cheating husband's life and watching him bleed out over my couch and carpet kept me awake all night. Other than that, I have slept just fine throughout the night every single day since he died.

"How are you holding up, honey?" Susan asks while pouring two cups of hot coffee for each of us. I prefer an iced coffee instead since it is about ninety degrees outside with a hundred percent humidity, but I'll keep my preferences to myself in this moment.

Oh, Susan, if you only knew how well I'm holding up. I feel better than I have ever felt in a while.

"I'm doing okay, I guess. Best as I possibly can be in the moment. This is the first time I've left the house in days. It's just weird not having him at home, knowing he's gone," I shudder. "It's so hard to even walk in the living room. I can barely look in its direction. Whenever I pass by, I run toward the kitchen or toward the stairs like... like someone is chasing me. Kind of like a flight response. It's crazy. Like, I can't face the room yet even though it's essential for me to pass by it whenever I go downstairs or in the kitchen. Did you know the police left me to clean up after the crime scene people left and took him? The coroners just took his body and left me to clean up after him. All that blood... It was traumatizing."

That part is true. Not about running past the living room. I walk by just fine. Sometimes I take a second to admire the living room and think about what I have accomplished, remembering his dead body and embracing how well I got the job done. The part about having to clean up his mess is true though. Just not the traumatizing part. The police took my statement, never bothered to treat me like a suspect since Sienna clearly did it (kudos to me), then left me alone with all that blood. It took me hours to clean everything all up. But instead of rage cleaning as I would normally do when I was feeling stressed, I cleaned out of pleasure. Who knew there could be such a thing?!

"That must have been so traumatizing. This whole experience is... it's just heartbreaking. I didn't know he was... he was unfaithful to you, dear. I'm so sorry," she cries, her eyes lost in her coffee. "I can't believe he's gone." This time, she wails like an annoying newborn.

Yes, he is gone. Dead. Buried six feet deep where he belongs.

Well, he will be buried soon after the funeral that I have to set up in a few days. That's when I'll really have to tap into my new role of the grieving widow. After that, all this acting can go away. I can't wait because it's already getting to be a little exhausting.

"I know, I know," is all I can muster while drinking another gulp of my coffee. The heat has dissipated and the coffee is actually quite tasty with a hint of chocolate and vanilla flavoring; my favorite type of latte.

Did Susan know this is my favorite flavor combination or is this a coincidence? Or did Jordan tell her what my favorite coffee is? Did he even know how I like my coffee? Who the hell knows?!

Even though Susan is still only a few inches beside me, her voice is becoming distant. Why does she sound far away?

Suddenly, the air feels warm. Sweat drips down my forehead. That's strange because this coffee is lukewarm now. My skin is boiling...

When did the temperature in the room become so hot? What happened to the A/C?

I take another sip of the coffee, surprised that I've gulped half of my drink down already.

But it's getting hard to swallow.

Something is stuck in my throat; it feels tight...

Can't breathe...

Was there a bug in my drink? I'm trying to spit it out, but nothing is coming out of my mouth. My throat feels like it's closing...

The room is spinning...

No, Susan is spinning... Is she smiling?

Something is wrong.

Something feels *really* wrong with me.

I should get up and run some water on my face. I'm probably dizzy from not eating yet today.

But the moment my feet touch the floor, the table seems to get closer. My attempt to stop it from hitting my face is short lived. The table connects with my nose. My head slams against the hard wood.

My vision becomes blurred.

My gasps for air become frantic.

Why is it so difficult to lift my head up?

Why is my face on the table?

Why can't I catch my breath?

"This is for taking my only son away from me, you bitch." Susan's words are clear, not as distant anymore. Her hot breath grazes my ear as she speaks, viciousness and a sense of accomplishment in her tone.

"When you told me some other woman murdered my beloved son in his own living room, I knew you lied because Jordan told me that you two were going out for dinner that night. You little bitch, you forgot how close my son and I were. He told me everything. I know you killed him and now you get what you deserve. Now I can watch you suffer. Just like you probably watched my son suffer in pain before his death, you can suffer in your own death, too."

Through my blurred vision, Susan's devious smile shines bright at me.

3 6

It was only right to avenge the death of my son. Even though killing his selfish wife will not bring Jordan back to me, it was all I could do. Jordan would be proud of me for making Lily suffer in her final moments. She got what she deserved.

Allowing Lily to rot in prison was not good enough punishment for murdering my son. That process would have taken too long to get her arrested, booked, and charged. I have no patience for lawyers and trials which could take months, and I also do not have enough evidence against Lily to prove she killed Jordan. Not without implicating my son of his sin in the past. Even though he is already gone, his secret will remain safe with me.

Jordan told me that Lily's brother found out about Jerry which meant Lily must've known about him too, so when my son told me that he had to get rid of him, I understood. But when Lily told me about Jordan's affair and his tragic death, I knew she killed him. She is not a good liar and her tears were pitiful.

My son was not unfaithful. A killer, yes. But only when he needed to be. Only when he had to defend me and look out for himself.

If it hadn't been for Lily's little brother eavesdropping on mine and Jordan's conversation, he would not have heard about Jerry and Lily wouldn't be dead right now. Mike not only caused his own death, but his sister's too. All for being nosey.

I loved my daughter in law. Never fully trusted her though. Especially her squirrely brother. Although we never met, Mike did not sound like a likeable person from the things Jordan told me about him. My son didn't like the guy, so neither did I. That was enough for me. We did not have to meet to get to know each other.

This was the best way to get rid of Lily. She deserved to choke on the pills that I crushed up and put in her coffee while coming to the realization that someone of the unexpected is killing her—just as she did to my son. She underestimated my motherly capabilities and took me for a fool. I hope she realized her mistakes in the end. If Jordan were still alive, he would be so proud of the way I handled things.

Now that Lily is dead, it is time to call the police and tell them she took too many of my prescription pills when I was in the kitchen making us coffee. She was so depressed about her husband's infidelity and tragic death that she ransacked my bathroom cabinet and took a handful of my pills when I wasn't looking.

Even after Jordan's betrayal, her love for him ran so deep, she couldn't live without him. What a twisted love story.

Acknowledgments

Thank you to my husband and my father for always being my first readers and honestly giving me their input on my stories.

To my family, anyone who supports me and to those who always buy every single one of my books regardless of whether they read them or not, those who provide honest reviews, and anyone who I force to answer my ridiculous questions to make the settings and characters come to life; I absolutely love and appreciate all of you.

To my ARC TEAM – You are amazing and so patient with me. I am forever grateful for your honesty and promotional work.

About the Author

Sara Kate with a K writes crime fiction, psychological, and survival thriller and mystery books in her RV out of South Florida. Aside from writing, she enjoys rollerblading, photography, painting, and anything thriller/mystery related.

INSTAGRAM.COM/SARAKATEAUTHOR
FACEBOOK.COM/SARAKATEAUTHOR
GOODREADS.COM/SARAKATEAUTHOR
BOOKBUB.COM/SARAKATEAUTHOR

BOOKS BY THE AUTHOR

FIND THESE BOOKS ON KINDLE, IN PAPERBACK & IN AUDIO.

THE WOMAN I BEFRIENDED: (Book 1 in "THE WOMAN" SERIES): *Several missing men. A suspicious neighbor. A pattern only Ellie sees.*

THE WOMAN I WANT DEAD: (Book 2 in "THE WOMAN" SERIES): *A cat and mouse serial killer thriller.*

HE THOUGHT I WAS HIS: *A psychological stalker thriller.*

EVERYTHING LED ME TO YOU: *A new adult romantic crime mystery/thriller.*

ZOEY'S MEMORY: *A medical mental health mystery.*

WE SHOULDN'T HAVE COME HERE: *A tropical storm thriller.*

THE UNSEEN AND UNINVITED: *A thriller short story on kindle unlimited.*

TWISTED VOWS: *A deadly marriage of lies and revenge.*

You can find Sara Kate's books on Amazon, Barnes & Noble, Walmart, Target, Books-a-million, and other store retailers!

You can also request any of her books to be stocked in your local independent bookstores.

If you enjoyed this book, I'd love to hear your thoughts in a review on Barnes & Noble and Amazon.